Will they...?

Won't they...?

Can they...?

The possibility of parenthood: for some couples
it's a seemingly impossible dream.
For others, it's an unexpected surprise....
Or perhaps it's a planned pregnancy
that brings a husband and wife closer together...
or turns their marriage upside down?

One thing is for sure, life will never be the same
when they find themselves having a baby...maybe!

This emotionally compelling miniseries
from Harlequin Romance® will warm your heart
and bring a tear to your eye....

Look out for
Their Doorstep Baby (#3718)
by Barbara Hannay
On sale September 2002

Grace Green grew up in Scotland but later emigrated to Canada with her husband and children. They settled in "Beautiful Super Natural B.C." and Grace now lives in a house just minutes from ocean, beaches, mountains and rain forest. She makes no secret of her favorite occupation—her bumper sticker reads: I'd Rather Be Writing Romance! Grace also enjoys walking the seawall, gardening, getting together with other authors...and watching her characters come to life, because she knows that once they do, they will take over and write her stories for her.

Books by Grace Green

HARLEQUIN ROMANCE®

3622—THE BABY PROJECT
3658—TWINS INCLUDED!
3706—THE NANNY'S SECRET*

*Linked to The Pregnancy Plan

THE PREGNANCY PLAN

Grace Green

TORONTO • NEW YORK • LONDON
AMSTERDAM • PARIS • SYDNEY • HAMBURG
STOCKHOLM • ATHENS • TOKYO • MILAN • MADRID
PRAGUE • WARSAW • BUDAPEST • AUCKLAND

For John

ISBN 0-373-03714-7

THE PREGNANCY PLAN

First North American Publication 2002.

This edition published by arrangement with Harlequin Books S.A.

Visit us at www.eHarlequin.com

Printed in U.S.A.

CHAPTER ONE

SHE came to him in the garden, on a morning gray with fog.

"The decision is yours, darling." Tears shimmered in her eyes. "But you must make it soon." Her voice caught. "This waiting...it's breaking my heart..."

Dermid ached to hold her, to comfort her, but even as he reached for her, she began to slip away.

"Wait!" he called, panicking. "Alice, wait!"

But she was already disappearing into the mist, the loose sleeves of her cloud-white dress billowing out behind her like angel wings floating her heavenward.

"Alice!" he cried again and tried to follow her, but the mist snaked wet tendrils around him, binding him—

"Dad!" A shake on his arm, a child's low urgent voice. *"Dad!"*

He groaned, and jerked from his nightmare, he came slowly, blearily...gratefully...awake.

Jack stood by the bed, in his unironed flannel pyjamas, his brown hair tufted, his hazel eyes anxious—far too anxious, Dermid thought with a pang of guilt—for a boy who had yet to celebrate his fifth birthday.

Leaning up on one elbow, clearing the rust of sleep from his throat, he said, "Sorry, son. Did I wake you?"

"You were shouting *really* loud. Was it bad?"

"It's been worse."

"But the same old nightmare?"

"Yup, same old one. And no, don't ask, I'm not going to tell you what it's about. Someday I will, when you're old enough to handle it." Dermid swung his long legs over the edge of the bed. "But right now—"

"But right now it would give me nightmares, too."

"You got it."

Dermid stood, and setting a firm hand on his son's shoulders, walked him to the window. "Now enough about nightmares. Will you just look at that morning out there?" The sun, an explosion of fire atop Vancouver Island's snowcapped Mountain Range, promised an unusually dazzling late-May day. "It's going to be a scorcher."

"Too bad we have to spend half of it on the ferry!"

"Don't you want to go over to the Lower Mainland to see your new cousin being christened?"

"I'd rather stay here on the ranch and help Arthur look after the animals."

"I'm not much of a party man myself, son, but we have to make the effort when it comes to family occasions."

They weren't really his family, only by marriage. They were Alice's family. But he was fond of them all. Except for Lacey. Lacey left him cold…because Lacey, herself, was cold. Superficial. Useless. Oh, she was decorative, he wasn't denying that, but useless. A pretty ornament. That was all. A bauble. She was

Alice's sister, but as unlike Alice as two women could have been.

Alice. He'd wanted to shut himself away from the outside world after she died, but for Jack's sake he couldn't. And for Jack's sake, he'd remained in close contact with his in-laws these past three years, although being with them only refreshed his grief and made it more difficult to put the past behind him. Not that he had a hope in hell of putting the past behind him until he found the courage to end the situation that was bedeviling him—

"Dad, do we *have* to go?"

"Yeah." Dermid stared out over the gardens below—Alice's gardens, once lovingly cared for as he himself had been and now—like himself!—sadly abandoned. "I need to talk to your uncle Jordan about something."

"Couldn't you do that over the phone?"

Dermid lifted his gaze beyond the gardens, to the pastures beyond. Over seventy acres, home to his herd of alpacas and llamas. "No, this is something really important, something I have to discuss face-to-face."

"You make it sound like a matter of life or death!"

But Jack had lost interest in the conversation as a lanky figure loped into view from the main barn.

"There's Arthur, I'm gonna get dressed and go help him muck out the shelters."

As Jack dashed away, his earlier comment echoed in Dermid's head and he felt a wave of despair.

Little did his son know how accurately he had assessed the situation, for the dilemma facing him truly was a matter of life or death.

And the decision he had to make—the one that had been giving him nightmares now for so very many months—was surely the cruelest that any man could ever have to face.

"Lacey, thank goodness you're here!"

Lacey Maxwell switched off the engine of her silver convertible. Taking the key from the ignition, she looked questioningly at her sister-in-law Felicity who had run down Deerhaven's front steps and was hurrying to the car.

Felicity came to a breathless stop just as Lacey was about to drop her keys into her gray leather bag.

"Don't put those away, Lace!"

"No?" Lacey paused, her slender crimson-tipped fingers splayed over the bag.

"I need to ask you a favor. Dermid called from the ferry a while ago to say there had been a long delay at Departure Bay so to save time he'd left the car at Nanaimo and he and Jack were on their way over as foot passengers. Jordan said he'd pick him up at Horseshoe Bay but he's been detained at the office so—"

"So you want me to do the honors."

"Would you, Lacey? I'd go myself, but it's time for the baby's feed and—"

"Say no more. It'll be my pleasure."

"You're a godsend!" Flicking back her blond braid,

Felicity glanced at her watch. "If you leave right now, you'll be there just as the ferry docks."

Lacey slipped her key into the ignition. "This is going to be fun. It'll make the laird beholden to me and he won't like that one little bit!"

"Lacey..."

"Mmm?" Lacey's smile was mischievous.

"Don't be too hard on him, will you?"

"I'll try my best, but he really does bring out the worst in me! Male chauvinists always do, and he's the most flagrant offender I've ever come across."

Felicity chuckled, a melodious infectious sound that made Lacey chuckle, too.

And as she spun her convertible away down the driveway, she thought—as she so often did—how lucky her brother Jordan was to have found such a perfect mate.

His first marriage had been a disaster. His wife Marla had been a hard and selfish woman who had for many years been unfaithful to him. After her death, Jordan had met and fallen deeply in love with Felicity, who had not only been his daughter Mandy's caregiver since infancy, she'd been more of a mother to Mandy than Marla had ever been. And after their marriage, Felicity had gone on to produce two darling boys, Todd and Andrew, and a baby girl, Verity, who was going to be the star of today's christening party.

It was going to be a lovely family get-together, Lacey mused as she raced the car along the Sea to Sky Highway toward the ferry terminal at Horseshoe Bay;

the only fly in the ointment being, of course, Dermid Andrew McTaggart.

And of course he wasn't really family. Only by marriage. His family—his parents and two brothers and a slew of other relatives—lived in Scotland. And as far as Lacey was concerned, that was where he should have stayed, with the rest of his clan!

He had never liked her.

She had been prepared to like him, as she'd have been prepared to like any man her sister had loved because she herself had adored Alice. But the blinkered Scot hadn't given her a chance. As far as he was concerned, models were vain empty creatures and he had no time for them.

And she certainly hadn't been about to grovel for his approval. She was neither vain nor empty but she had more than her fair share of pride. And if there was ever to be an end to the cold war between her and Dermid McTaggart, he would have to make the first move.

And the earth, she thought with a dry smile, was more likely to move first!

"I thought Uncle Jordan was going to meet us." Jack looked around anxiously. "Where is he?"

The village of Horseshoe Bay on this blistering hot day was jammed with tourists, buses, cabs, vehicles of all sorts. Holidaymakers thronged the sidewalks, window-shopping—looking at jade jewelry, carved totem poles, Vancouver sweatshirts. Others licked ice-cream cones and wandered aimlessly, enjoying the sea breeze and the spectacular view—the yachts bobbing in the marina; the vast white B.C. Ferry; the shimmering blue ocean.

"Your uncle's probably driving around trying to find a parking spot. We'd best stand right here, and wait for him. He'll—"

"Hello, Dermid."

The voice came from behind him, but he'd have recognized it anywhere. Light, feminine, flippant. Challenging.

He turned, and there she was. His sparring partner. Stunning as ever, in a crisp white shirt and icy-blue linen slacks. And looking, amid the throng of perspiring sun-baked tourists, as cool as an iced drink in the desert.

"Lacey." His tone was faintly mocking. "Are you our chauffeur?"

"Jordan sends his apologies, he couldn't get away." She shifted her attention to Jack, who was gazing up at her with the expression of a lovesick swain. "Jack, it's great to see you."

"You, too, Aunt Lacey!"

"I've got something for you, darling. A present. I got it in France when I was there last week..."

Dermid felt a sense of irritation as he watched them chat.

She had a way with men, no doubt about it. And with boys. She never talked down to Jack, never had; she always treated him like an adult. And he, poor sod, had been mad about her from the time his newborn eyes could focus, and he could see that sheet of ink-black hair, those green cat-eyes and that impossibly flawless creamy skin. Soon the poor kid would be old enough to notice the endless legs, the seductive walk, the sexy rear end, the—

"Well, Dermid, shall we go?" She swung away toward the street, the movement sending a drift of her perfume into his space. To follow her, he had to walk through the mingled scent of gardenia petals and enough musk to make a red-blooded male howl at the moon!

"I'm parked over here." With self-assurance in every elegant step, she led the way into the parking lot. And stopped by her silver convertible, which had the top down.

"Your car is so cool, Aunt Lacey!" Jack's eyes glowed with excitement. "Can I sit in front with you?"

"I don't see why not," she said gaily. "If your father doesn't mind?"

"Do you, Dad?"

"No," he growled.

And within seconds they were on their way out of the parking lot and on their way up to the highway…the driver's hair flying out behind her with a life of its own.

She and Jack talked to each other nonstop. Occasionally she'd call over her shoulder, "Are you okay back there?" and he'd answer with a curt "Yes!"

Once he caught a glimpse of her in the rearview mirror, looking at him. For just a second, their eyes locked, before she quickly fixed hers on the road again; but in that fleeting exchange he thought he detected not only vulnerability, but a look of wistful wisdom.

And he knew only too well that he must have been mistaken, for Lacey Maxwell was neither vulnerable nor wistful nor wise.

What she was, was a beautiful bore.

But she'd done him a favor by coming to pick him up...and although given a choice he'd rather have walked, he was now beholden to her.

And the sooner he paid that debt, the happier he'd be.

So when they approached the next exit, he leaned forward and yelled, into the streaming ribbons of her black hair, "Could you stop by at the Caulfeild mall?"

She nodded. And putting out her signal, drove onto the exit ramp.

The shopping center was just minutes from the highway, and as soon as she'd parked, he jumped out.

"I'll be right back."

He'd intended buying flowers, but at the last moment he changed his mind and bought a box of Belgian chocolates instead. The woman could do with a bit of beef on her!

When he walked back toward the car, he could see she and Jack were talking. They didn't notice him approach, but he could hear Jack's eager voice from twenty feet away.

"...and me and my dad aren't big on family parties, and I told him I'd have rather stayed home and mucked about on the ranch than come over here and act gaga over some baby—''

He broke off as he noticed his father.

''Oh, hi, Dad. I was just telling Aunt Lacey that—''

''Yeah, I heard.''

Lacey looked up at him, her expression amused. ''Your son and I are on the same wavelength when it comes to babies—we agree they're no fun to be around till they're toilet-trained and able to have a decent conversation.''

''Aunt Lacey thinks they're messy and noisy and need attention 24-7...24-7, Dad. Aunt Lacey says that means twenty-four hours a day, seven days a week.''

''In other words, a full-time job.'' Dermid got into the back seat. And added, as Lacey turned around in her seat to look at him, ''A bit more exhausting, I'd imagine, and certainly more fulfilling, than spending an hour or two, here or there, leaning against a coconut palm and getting your picture taken for some glossy magazine! How would you describe *your* job, Lacey? Maybe a 3-2?''

Her green eyes, which had been twinkling with laughter, now clouded over. And he got the sense that he'd doused whatever joy she'd been feeling in the day.

Lips compressed, she turned from him, flicked the key in the ignition, and set the car in motion.

Jack appeared to have noticed the clashing vibrations, for he sank, obviously subdued, back in his seat.

And neither he, nor his aunt, spoke one more word to him or to each other for the rest of the journey.

* * *

Deerhaven, the Maxwell's five-bedroom home, stood high on the slopes of West Vancouver. With a panoramic view of the ocean, it sat in parklike grounds, with a swimming pool, a white-painted cabana, and a play area for the children.

Lacey had her own condo a few minutes away, but every chance she got, she visited Deerhaven. Over the years, Felicity had become her closest friend…but there was one secret Lacey kept from Felicity, and it concerned Dermid.

Felicity thought highly of her brother-in-law, and both she and Jordan considered the ongoing thrust-and-parry between him and Lacey to be harmless. What neither of them knew was that in recent months, Dermid's put-downs had become more cutting.

And Lacey was afraid that if she wasn't careful she'd let her guard down and he'd see that he was drawing blood.

Today's snide comment had been particularly hurtful.

"How would you describe your job, Lacey? Maybe 3-2?"

At his sarcastic comment, all her joy in the day had faded. And she'd felt a surge of resentment. He considered a model's life to be one of glamour and ease; little did he know that sometimes she was so exhausted she almost fell apart. Not only was she constantly traveling, the shoots themselves were extremely stressful, as were the fashion shows in Milan, Paris, London…

Stifling a sigh, she pushed all her negative thoughts aside as she drew her car to a halt in front of Deerhaven. She was *not* going to let Dermid's unpleasant jabs dampen her mood; she had planned to have a good time at today's party and that was exactly what she was going to do.

Jack opened his seat belt buckle. "Dad, can I go around the back and see if my cousins are out there?"

"Sure, go ahead."

He and Lacey walked toward the front door together. When they reached the stoop, he turned and looked out over the ocean.

"Some view," he murmured, almost to himself.

Lacey followed his gaze, and saw that seven freighters sat waiting to be loaded with grain, and dozens of yachts dotted the waters, while a few speedboats raced around.

"Yes, it's fabulous."

Lacey glanced up at him, and as she did, she could—as always—easily see why her sister had fallen in love with him. With his dark auburn hair, rugged features, and sexy mouth, Dermid McTaggart really was a very attractive man.

It was too bad he didn't have a personality to match!

Lacey had her own key to Deerhaven, and taking it out, she unlocked the door. He followed her into the foyer.

From upstairs came the fretty cry of a baby.

Lacey moved over to the foot of the stairs. "Fliss, we're here!"

A few seconds later, Felicity appeared on the landing. She beamed down at them.

"Hi, Dermid, delighted you could make it. Where's Jack?"

"He went round the back to look for his cousins."

"Good, they're playing there with Shauna—my baby-sitter from next door. Jordan called, he's on his way home. I'm just going to put Verity down for a nap and we'll have a drink before lunch. We've loads of time, the christening's not till two-thirty."

"Anything I can do to help?" Lacey asked.

"You're such a whizz at setting the table, would you mind...?"

"Not at all."

"And Dermid, could you take Andrew's high chair from the kitchen and set it up in the dining room?"

"Sure."

As Felicity went back to the nursery, Dermid ambled off and Lacey went into the dining room.

She set the table, using Felicity's best linen and silver and crystal, and then taking white linen napkins from the drawer, she fashioned them into intricate swans and set them in the glasses by each place mat, smiling to herself as she stood back to admire her handiwork.

She detested housecleaning and she couldn't cook but there was no denying she could set a mean table.

Dermid, on the other hand, hadn't even managed to bring through the high chair!

As she made her way to the kitchen to take him to task, she heard Jordan's voice.

"...yes of course we can talk about it," he was saying.

"Later," Dermid said. "After the party's over. It's private, Jordan, and personal. A family matter."

"But if it has to do with Alice, as you said, shouldn't Lacey be involved, too?"

"No!" Dermid's tone was sharp. "She's the last person whose input I'd want on this. Jordan, I've struggled with this situation for far too long and I have to make a decision. At least, I've made my decision, and what I need from you is support—"

Lacey became aware of footsteps running down the stairs. And realizing, with dismay, that she'd been eavesdropping, she hurried back to the foyer and arrived there just as Felicity reached the foot of the stairs.

"You've set the table?" her sister-in-law asked.

"Mmm. Come along and see my swans!"

But though she managed to put on a cheerful face, Lacey felt edgy and upset.

What was going on in her brother-in-law's life that required him to ask Jordan for support?

It was clear he didn't want *her* to know anything about it. And that made her furious. She was a Maxwell, too, and if it was a family matter concerning Alice, then Dermid McTaggart had no business trying to shut her out!

One way or another, she promised herself, she would get to the bottom of it!

CHAPTER TWO

THE christening took place outdoors at Deerhaven, the sunken rose garden made a perfect setting and Jordan and Felicity looked blissfully happy.

"I think," the minister said later in the afternoon, before he left, "that everything went off rather well." His eyes twinkled. "Baby Verity is blessed with a remarkable pair of lungs."

Jordan laughed, saying "She may well be a budding opera singer!" as he walked the minister into the house from the patio, where the adults had enjoyed champagne and tea and a slice of Felicity's delicious homemade white-chocolate christening cake after the ceremony.

Felicity had gone upstairs to put the baby down for a nap and the other children were having a picnic in the play area...which left Dermid alone on the patio with Lacey.

He noticed that though she'd taken an active part in the conversation while the minister was present, now she lay back in her cushioned lounger and closed her eyes.

Shutting him out.

And he could hardly blame her. Ever since she'd picked him up at the ferry, some perverse impulse had driven him to snipe at her. That comment he'd made, about her job being a "3-2" had been totally uncalled for. So what if she lived an easy glamorous life, one that was shallow and useless? Just because he despised that kind of nonproductive existence was no excuse for taking potshots at her. But what had impelled him into goading her further today had been the fact that she hadn't responded with her usual acerbity. And what satisfaction was there in needling someone who refused to be needled!

She looked, right now, totally oblivious to him. She also looked as if she were posing for some fashion spread. Elegance personified.

But her silk dress, which she'd changed into before the ceremony—black with a pattern of tiny white flowers— probably cost more than one of his prize alpacas!

"I can see," she drawled, "by the derisive curl of your lip, that you're thinking a nasty thought about me."

She'd barely raised her eyelids but he could detect a challenging glitter from beneath the coal-dark lashes.

She tilted her head, provocatively. "Go ahead," she said. "Spit it out. It can't be good for you, to keep all that poison bubbling inside."

He decided to accept the challenge. "I was just thinking," he said lazily, "that your dress probably cost more than one of my prize alpacas."

"Yes," she said, "I shouldn't be surprised if it did. And you were probably thinking, also, what a useless life I lead, compared with one of your beloved beasts."

He glanced at the table. "It did occur to me," he murmured, "that if Alice had still been here, she'd have whipped all these dishes and glasses inside and be cleaning up in the kitchen, to take some of the load off Felicity."

Now he was being mean, and he didn't like it—or himself—one bit. He saw her stiffen. But when she spoke, instead of an angry retort, he got a restrained reply.

"I know you miss Alice, but you won't ever get to me by holding her up as an example—I'm in total agreement that she was one in a million. I know she meant the world to you, and I know how unhappy you've been since she died. And I'm guessing you're stuck at the 'anger' stage of your grief. If it helps to use me as a whipping boy, feel free to continue."

The patio doors behind her slid open and Felicity came out, with Jordan following.

As casually as if she and Dermid hadn't been spatting, Lacey looked up at Felicity and said in a pleasant tone, "Did you get the baby settled?"

"Mmm, she's out like a light. Wasn't she sweet, in her christening gown?"

"She was adorable." Lacey swung herself gracefully up from her chaise. "Now I'm going out to the car to fetch the presents I brought for the children. Will you come and give me a hand?"

"Of course. But you shouldn't have—"

"I know, I spoil them...but since I have no children of my own, just indulge me!"

"By the way," her brother said, "what happened with that English guy who chased you all over Europe? The one with the castle in Wiltshire."

"Sir Harry? Oh, I ditched him when he told me he expected me to give up my career when we married, and start having babies—lots of 'em!—right away. Male chauvinism run riot! Besides, can you imagine yours truly coping with dirty diapers and bottles of formula and sleepless nights...not to mention having to lumber around like an elephant for the best part of nine months!" She gave an elegant shudder. "I think not!"

"Being pregnant is wonderful!" Felicity protested. "I adored it...and would have quite happily gone on and had another new baby every couple of years till I was too old to have anymore!"

"Which is why after Verity was born," her husband reminded her with a warm chuckle, "we both agreed that four were enough!"

Dermid had remained quiet during the talk of babies, but after Lacey and Felicity left the patio, he said,

"Jordan, do you think we could discuss that matter now, the one I mentioned earlier?"

"Sure," Jordan said. "Let's go into my study, where we won't be disturbed."

Lacey had brought new swimsuits for the children, and a colorful beach ball for each of them.

"Can we go in the pool now, Mom?" Eight-year-old Mandy waved her new lemon-yellow bikini in the air.

"Can we, Mom?" echoed Todd, two, and Andrew, four, as they gleefully rolled their new blue-and-green striped balls across the carpet in the den, setting RJ, the cat, scurrying for cover.

"Please, Aunt Felicity?" Jack loved to swim with his Dad in the swimming hole on their property, but it was always a treat to swim in the blue-tiled pool at Deerhaven.

"Let's *all* go for a swim!" Lacey said. "It's so hot today, it'll be fabulous to cool off. Do let's," she urged Felicity. "You can take the baby monitor with you."

"I really should clean up first," Felicity said.

"I'll help," Lacey offered, but Felicity shook her head.

"No you go ahead, I'll come out when I'm finished."

"My bikini's still in the laundry room?"

"Mmm, where you left it last time. And could you bring up the beach towels?" Felicity turned to Mandy. "Honey, will you get the sunscreen and then all of you wait here till Aunt Lacey comes back, and she'll take you outside to the cabana to get changed and put on the suntan lotion."

Within minutes Lacey was herding them all outside. And soon they were all in the water.

Jack and Andrew, both strong swimmers, immediately struck out across the pool toward the deep end, punching their beach balls ahead of them, while Mandy and Lacey played in the shallow end with Todd.

Felicity turned up after about twenty minutes. She

was carrying a tray, with a pitcher of lemonade, a stack of plastic glasses, and the baby monitor. Setting the tray and monitor on the picnic table by the pool, she stood for a moment, adjusting the straps of her amethyst one-piece swimsuit.

"You're looking terrific," Lacey called. "You've put on a few pounds with this last baby, but it suits you."

"Thanks, Lacey! So...where did Jordan and Dermid disappear to?"

"I don't know. I haven't seen them since you and I went out to the car to get the presents."

Just as Felicity made to jump into the water, Todd started to fuss.

"Want a drink! Want out!"

Mandy had been holding him; now she carried him to the steps and her mother reached down and hoisted him up.

"A woman's work," Felicity said with a laugh, "is never done!"

Mandy retrieved her beach ball which had drifted away, and shouted, "Catch, Aunt Lacey!"

For the next while, Lacey played with Mandy, until Felicity interrupted them.

"Lacey, can you come out? I need to talk to you."

She sounded so serious, Lacey felt a jolt of surprise; surprise that changed to concern when she saw her sister-in-law's unhappy expression.

"And Mandy—" Felicity took Todd's empty glass from him "—will you come out, too, and take Todd over to the cabana and get him changed? I think he's ready for a nap and I want to have a chat with Aunt Lacey.''

Lacey climbed up the steps, and wringing out her sodden hair, walked over to Felicity. She waited till Mandy had taken Todd to the cabana before saying anxiously,

''What's wrong, Fliss?''

''Oh, Lacey, it's so sad. When I tell you, I know you'll be so upset—'' She broke off as Jordan came out of the house. ''Shh,'' she whispered. ''I can't tell you just now, not till after Dermid's gone. Please don't say anything to Jordan. Not yet.''

The pool area was surrounded by chain link fencing, and as Jordan opened the gate, he called,

''Hey, Jack, come on out now. You and your dad have to leave in about ten minutes.''

''Are you going to drive him?'' Felicity asked.

''No, I'm afraid I have to go back to the office...''

Jordan was manager of one of the North Shore's top real estate firms, and Sunday, at this time of year, was always one of the agency's busiest days.

''...but,'' he added, ''I said you'd drive him, Lace. Okay?''

Lacey bit her tongue. ''Sure, no problem.''

Jordan turned toward the house. ''Ah, here he is.''

Jack clambered out of the pool and ran to his father. ''Do we *have* to go now?'' he asked. ''Can't we stay for a while longer?''

''No,'' Dermid said. ''It's time we were going.''

"Aw!" Jack pulled a long face. "I was having a good time..."

"Why don't you let him stay for a few days?" Felicity suggested. "You could come back for him on the weekend."

Dermid turned to Jack. "Do you want to stay on, on your own?" The child never had before.

"Sure! Thanks, Dad! Thanks, Aunt Felicity." And without further ado, Jack tore off and yelling to his cousins, "I'm staying!" he plunged into the water again.

Smiling, Jordan turned to his brother-in-law. "So Lace will drive you to the ferry, whenever you're ready."

Dermid's eyes met Lacey's. His were cool. "Thanks," he said, "but I've called a cab."

Lacey lifted one shoulder in a careless shrug. "Fine." What a *boor* the man was!

"Well, guys, I'll have to go now," Jordan said. "Thanks for coming over, Dermid. I know this isn't your kind of 'do,' but Fliss and I have always appreciated the effort you've made to keep Jack in close touch with his cousins."

"We know it must have been hard at first, coming here without Alice." Felicity patted his arm. "But I hope it's become easier, with time."

Dermid said, "Alice would have wanted it this way."

"You're right, she would," Jordan said, giving

Felicity a warm kiss goodbye. "Okay, folks, I'm off. Bye, all!"

Once he'd gone, Dermid stood chatting with Felicity for a few minutes, until they heard the toot of a car horn.

"That'll be your cab." Felicity turned to Lacey. "Will you see Dermid out, Lace? I don't want to leave the children alone in the pool."

"Not necessary," Dermid said quickly. "I can see myself out—"

"Oh, but I *insist!*" Lacey said, with exaggerated graciousness. "My list of faults is long enough without adding bad manners to it!"

And with her nose in the air, she led him into the house and out through the foyer.

As they passed the hallstand, she noticed, sitting on it, the bag containing whatever it was that Dermid had bought at the Caulfeild Mall. He'd set it there when he'd come in that morning.

She indicated it, and said, "Is that for Felicity? Did you forget to give it to her?"

He paused in the open doorway. "It's for you."

"For *me?*"

Frowning, she scooped up the bag and looked inside and saw a lovely box of very expensive Belgian chocolates.

Taken completely by surprise, she said, "Thank you, Dermid! I have such a weakness for chocolate and these are my favorites!" So, the man had a soft spot after all. Teasingly she said, "What *is* this? A peace offering?"

His eyes were beautiful and unique in color—the whisky brown of a Highland stream, Alice used to say. But those same eyes which had glowed with love when he looked at his wife, now flattened with denial when he looked at his sister-in-law.

"It's a thank you," he said curtly. "For picking me up at Horseshoe Bay."

He could have slapped her and she wouldn't have felt more wounded. Or humiliated. But gritting her teeth, she swiftly rebounded from his nastiness.

"Of course," she said. "I should have known. I feel sorry for you, Dermid McTaggart. What a petty mind you do have! What I did was a favor. And a very small one at that. But could you accept it? Oh, no. No way. It would never do for the almighty McTaggart to be beholden to anyone, and certainly not to me. Well, I'd like to take your fancy Belgian chocolates and shove them…well, you can guess where. But I won't. Unlike you, I do possess some of the social graces, and I do know how to accept a gift!"

Before he could stop her, she reached up on her tiptoes and kissed him on the cheek.

Then standing back, she said, "Maybe that's not the way it's done where you come from, McTaggart, but that's the way it's done here. A smile, a thank you, and a friendly kiss. You know the old saying: while in Rome, do as the Romans do. I hope you'll remember it in future!"

With that, she whirled away, leaving him to see himself out...and good manners be damned!

Clouds had drifted in from the west and when Lacey returned to the garden, she felt a drop of rain on her arm.

Felicity said, "We're going to have a shower! I'll put Todd down for a nap and the other children can watch TV in the den while you and I have our talk."

By the time she had settled the children, a cloud had crept over the sun and the rain was sprinkling down.

"Let's sit on the patio," she said. "I'll roll down the awning."

As she rolled it down, she said, "It was too bad Sarah and the others came down with 'flu this week. They were looking forward to coming over for the party today."

"You're so lucky to have Sarah. And Gigi," she added, referring to Felicity's other sister, both of whom lived on Vancouver Island. "I miss Alice terribly. She was more than a wonderful older sister, she was like a mother to me—brought me up, as you know, after Mom died. And she was also my best friend."

"Dermid's best friend, too—I don't think I've ever seen two people so devoted to each other." She sighed. "Which brings me to what I have to tell you." She crossed the patio and sat down on one of the lawn chairs.

But when she gestured to Lacey to do the same, Lacey shook her head. She felt too restless to sit down.

"Before you start, Fliss, I have to confess that I may not be totally in the dark about what you're going to say. This morning, I accidentally eavesdropped while Dermid and Jordan were talking and I heard Dermid refer to a family matter and a decision Dermid had to make, and he asked Jordan for his support."

"Poor Dermid. With his Scottish pride, and his fierce independence, it couldn't have been easy for him to ask Jordan for anything! As for eavesdropping, I'm afraid I've been guilty of it, too. You see, after I set up the baby monitor at the pool, while I was giving Todd his lemonade I heard Jordan and Dermid talking. They were in the nursery, Jordan apparently checking on Verity—and he and Dermid were talking quietly...although it obviously didn't occur to either of them that they could be overheard."

"I should tell you, Fliss, Dermid made it clear to Jordan that he didn't want me involved in the situation."

"He may not want you involved, but I do think you ought to know. *Alice* would want you to know."

"Fliss, if you don't come to the point—"

"Sorry. Okay, here goes. You know that Dermid had a bout with cancer a long while ago, just after he and Alice were married, and that before he underwent radiation treatment, on the oncologist's advice he had some of his sperm frozen because it was possible the treatment would render him infertile...which, unhappily, it did."

''Yes, of course. And I know that later on, Jack was born from a frozen embryo.''

''Do you remember, Lacey, that Dermid and Alice had a second embryo, cryogenically frozen, and stored at that same clinic in Toronto—the embryo of a girl baby—and that Alice and Dermid looked forward to one day having that child—''

''But Alice died before they could.'' Lacey's throat felt suddenly tight. ''I often think of that little baby who'll never be born...I find it so sad, and it would have broken Alice's heart...'' Her voice trailed into silence.

All around, the rain was lashing down now. Lacey hadn't even noticed it getting heavier, and the afternoon had become bleak and cool and very dark.

She blinked away threatening tears, and saw Felicity rise from her seat. Her sister-in-law crossed over to her, took her hands and held them tight.

''Lacey, Dermid's been having nightmares. Alice has been coming to him, begging him to let her rest in peace. She wants closure. He wants closure, too. So...he's finally going to do the thing he's been putting off doing ever since Alice died. He's going to contact the fertility clinic in Toronto this week, and tell them he no longer wants the remaining embryo preserved.''

CHAPTER THREE

"HE SHOULD have told me!" Lacey glared at her brother. "Alice was my sister, too, I had every right to know what he was planning to do. He had no right to shut me out!"

Jordan made a placating gesture. "Honey, this has been very difficult for Dermid—"

"Of course it has, I'm not denying that. It must be breaking his heart, knowing that Alice's baby is there, just waiting for a chance to be born. But now she never will be!" Lacey felt her anger dissipating as sorrow took over. "Oh, Jordan, why does life have to be so cruel?"

He had nothing to say that would comfort her. He looked helplessly at Felicity, who looked back equally helplessly at him.

Lacey paced the sitting room. She crossed to the window, looked out in the pitch-dark night. Jordan had been very late getting home, but she couldn't settle until she'd had it out with him, had vented all the resentment she felt toward Dermid McTaggart.

Impatient, she whirled around now. "I still can't forgive him for not including me in his decision-making. I know he thinks I'm an airhead—"

"If he does," Jordan said, "you have only yourself

to blame. You've deliberately led him to believe you're a bit spacey—"

"Only because from the moment we met, he made it clear that he thought anyone who made a living the way I did must have the IQ of a gnat!"

"Let's not get sidetracked, Lace." Her brother's expression had become somber. "No matter how smart you are, what could you have contributed to our conversation? After all, the matter was simple. Dermid had already made his decision, and what he wanted from me, as Alice's brother, was my support...and that was all there was to it."

"No, I won't accept that!" Lacey's silver bracelets flashed in the light as she stuck her fists on her hips. "Three heads are better than two—and if you'd included me in your furtive little get-together, I might have come up with some other option."

"It wasn't furtive. It was private. Besides, what other option could you have come up with? All you could have suggested was that he delay the inevitable. The man's been having nightmares, Lace, for months! Leaving the situation the way it is, is not an option."

"So what's his next step?" Felicity asked.

"He's going to Toronto on Friday, to talk with the people at the clinic, tell them not to preserve the embryo any longer."

Felicity tsked. "Won't that be terribly hard on him—going back there, where he and Alice...?"

"Yeah, it'll be hard. But Dermid feels it's something he can't do by phone. He wants to do it in person—"

''There *is* another option.'' Lacey's voice had been quiet, but it stopped Jordan in his tracks.

He looked warily at her. ''There is?''

''Yes.'' Excitement welled up inside her. ''Dermid can hire a surrogate mother—she'd be a gestational carrier, actually, since she wouldn't have any genetic link to the child—to bear the baby for him!''

''I already suggested that to Dermid,'' Jordan said. ''This morning.''

''And?'' Lacey demanded. ''What did he say?''

''Emphatically 'No!'. He won't even consider it.''

''Is it the money issue?'' Felicity asked. ''He wouldn't feel comfortable paying someone to act as a host uterus?''

''It's nothing to do with money. I don't remember his exact words, but the gist of it was that making a baby was a family affair, and not something an outsider should ever be part of.'' Jordan shrugged. ''It is *not* an option.''

''He's a stubborn man, is the McTaggart.'' Lacey's excitement died. 'Well, that's that, then.'' She sat on the arm of her brother's chair. ''You were right, Jordan. I couldn't have contributed anything useful to your conversation. And now that the decision is made, sad as it is, we'll all just have to accept it.''

''It's particularly sad for *Dermid,*'' Felicity said. ''He won't ever be able to have another child, should he decide to remarry.''

There remained nothing more to say on the matter, and soon after, Lacey got up to leave.

"Are you going to be home for a while?" Jordan asked as he and Felicity walked her out to her car. "Or are you off on a shoot somewhere?"

"I'm going to be around for the next while, taking a bit of a break. But after that, I'm heavily committed for the next several months. And my agent's been making overtures to GloryB. They're going to be looking for a replacement for Kinga Koff—their GloryB girl—because she's getting married in the Fall and she's planning to retire."

"For their cosmetic line, then," Felicity said. "Oh, how thrilling!"

"Fingers crossed," Lacey said. "It's always been my dream, to be the face of GloryB!"

She smiled as she stood by her silver convertible and looked out over the dark waters of the inlet. "If it all works out, I may be asking you to find a house for me, Jordan. Something really deluxe, up here on the hill."

But as she drove away a few moments later, her smile faded and she was left with her thoughts. Desolate thoughts about Alice, and the baby who would never be born.

Alice had done so much for her after their mother died, and had made many huge sacrifices. Lacey had thanked her many times, but mere thanks had never seemed adequate.

If only, she reflected, with a sense of grief and great loss, she had ever been able to do something to repay her beloved sister, but the occasion had never arisen.

* * *

"Aunt Lacey, this is Jack speaking..."

Lacey stood in her kitchen, making coffee as she listened to her nephew's voice on her answering machine. She'd been in the shower and hadn't heard the phone ring, but now, on this gray Thursday morning, with her wet hair wrapped in a towel, she gave his message her attention.

"Aunt Lacey, nobody knows I'm phoning—I'm in Uncle Jordan's study, he's at work and Aunt Felicity's busy with the baby. Here's why I'm calling. Can you come and drive me home? I'm just itchin' to get back. So...will you call me if you can come? Please? Love, Jack."

Lacey gave a wry smile. Who could have resisted that earnest "Love, Jack"?

She phoned Deerhaven and when Felicity answered, she asked to talk to Jack. When he came on the line, she said, "I got your message, and I'd be happy to take you home. Can you be ready to leave in about an hour?"

"Sure! And thanks, Aunt Lacey!"

"Now talk to your aunt. Come clean, tell her you're homesick, she'll understand. And I'll pick you up at ten."

Jack was ready when she arrived at Deerhaven, and they drove straight out to Horseshoe Bay. The morning was still overcast, and by the time they boarded the ferry, rain was drizzling down.

But it cleared up after a while, and by the time they reached Nanaimo, sunshine and blue skies greeted them.

Jack had chattered happily on the ferry trip, but on the drive to the ranch, he lapsed into silence. Slumping back in his seat, he stared glumly out of the window.

"Is something wrong?" Lacey asked as they turned off the highway and onto the side road leading to the ranch. "I thought you'd be so excited to be home, but—"

"I am."

"You don't *sound* very excited!" She glanced at him and saw his little face was drawn down in lugubrious lines. "I know you wanted to surprise your dad, but maybe we should have called and told him you were coming back early—are you afraid he'll be away somewhere?"

Jack shook his head. "If he wasn't here, Arthur would be around. It's just...well, I'm glad to be back, but..."

"But what?"

"They're lucky," he muttered. "Mandy and Andrew and Todd and the baby. All these kids to play with, they'd never be lonely. I just wish I had a brother—or a sister—but I'm never going to have one. My dad was sick a long time ago and now he can't have any more kids. It sucks."

"I know," she said gently, "that it must be hard, being an only child. But at least you have cousins, and you get to see them quite often."

"Yeah," he said. "I guess."

But it was obvious he felt they were a poor second-best to actually having a brother or sister of his own.

By now they were approaching the house, and she saw Arthur emerge from the back door.

A confirmed bachelor and shy around women, the man had worked with Jordan for many years, and was now a permanent fixture at the ranch.

"Look," Lacey said, hoping to divert Jack from his forlorn musings. "There's Arthur!"

Jack bounced up in his seat, waving.

Arthur loped toward the car, and gave Lacey a respectful salute. "Hi, there, Ms. Maxwell."

Jack snapped open his seat belt. "Where's Dad?"

"Inside, throwin' a few things in a bag. He's going to Toronto, flyin' out from Vancouver this evenin'."

"I thought," Lacey said, "he was going on Friday?"

"Too impatient, he was, too restless, to wait."

"Arthur!" Jack opened his car door and hopped out. "Did Molly May have her cria yet?"

"Yup, yesterday, like clockwork. Cute as a button, too...your dad called her Molly Maybe."

Jack said, "I can't wait to see her—come on, Aunt Lacey. You gotta see this!"

Heavy rain must have fallen here earlier; the track was still muddy in places. But even if it had been dry, Lacey wouldn't have jumped at the chance to traipse off looking at animals. That had been Alice's life. It certainly wasn't *her* idea of a good time.

"No, thanks," she said. "I'll pass."

"Okay. But thanks for taking me over!" Jack ran around to her side of the car, and put up his arms for a hug.

She leaned over and gave him a warm one. "I enjoyed the trip," she said. "It's always fun to have an outing with such a cool young dude!"

Jack beamed with pleasure. Then turning to the ranch hand, he said, "Let's go, Arthur!"

Arthur put a hand on the boy's shoulder. "You'd better nip inside first and let your dad know you're back."

"Aunt Lacey will. Right, Aunt Lacey?"

She'd intended to leave without seeing Dermid. It still rankled that he hadn't included her in the private talk he'd had with Jordan. But Jack was hopping around impatiently, eyes eager as he waited for her response.

How could she refuse? "Yes, I'll tell him."

"Just go in," Arthur said. "The doorbell needs fixin', and he's upstairs, won't hear you if you knock."

While he and Jack headed off, she got out of the car and walked toward the house, stepping carefully so's not to muddy her cream leather pumps.

To her right was the terraced bank that Alice had transformed into a picturesque garden. While she'd been alive, it had been a joy to behold at this time of year; now weeds flourished, crowding out the once-vibrant perennials that Alice had so lovingly planted and tended.

But it wasn't only the garden that had a desolate air; the house itself looked sad. Paint was peeling off the green front door and the brass fittings cried out for a polish. Where once the windows would have been open to the fresh spring day, with crisply laundered curtains billowing in the breeze, now they were shut...closing out the world.

Lacey opened the door and walked into the entryway. Stepping over mud-caked boots, noting the grit on the formerly gleaming slate floor, she felt her spirits sink.

And they sank further as she looked around the front hall. This would break Alice's heart, she thought with a spurt of anger, if she could see it. The hall table was thick with dust, as were the pictures on the walls, and the carpet leading up the stairs was fuzzed with lint.

Tears stung her eyes. How *could* he! How could Dermid McTaggart have let Alice's cherished home fall into such a state of abandonment!

Dermid stepped out of the shower in his en suite bathroom, and whisking a towel from the floor, he ran it over his hair. Then tucking it around his waist, he swiped a hand over the steamed-up mirror, brushed his hair, and then threw the brush, along with his shaving gear, into the toilet bag he was going to take to Toronto with him.

Tomorrow, he was going to the clinic.

Tomorrow, he was going to do something that would make his heart ache for the rest of his life.

And after he'd signed the necessary papers, he reflected as he brushed his teeth, he'd no doubt feel like going to the nearest pub to drown his sorrows; but he wouldn't, because of Jack—

Someone hammered on his bedroom door.

Arthur? What did he want? And when had *he* ever knocked!

He turned off the tap and heard the knocking again. This time, it was even more demanding. And it was followed immediately by the sound of a voice he recognized, one that had him almost choking...then spitting out his toothpaste as if he'd discovered it contained arsenic.

Lacey Maxwell.

What the devil was she doing here!

Dropping his toothbrush on the countertop, he strode to the bathroom door and came to an abrupt halt.

There she was, in his bedroom, dressed in an indigo shirt and a cream miniskirt and cream shoes, with her black hair falling like a sheet of jet to her breasts.

And she was spitting mad.

"Didn't you hear me knock?" Her green eyes had a furious sparkle. "Are you *deaf?*"

He swallowed and the toothpaste made his throat feel raw. "What—" his tone was incredulous "—are *you* doing here?"

"How could you!" She glared at him. "How could you let this place go to rack and ruin. Alice would turn in her grave if—"

"I asked," he said grimly, "what you are doing here."

She sliced a hand through the air, the gesture angry and dismissive. "I brought Jack back. He was homesick. Though how he could be homesick for such a pigstye is utterly beyond me! How can you possibly justify what you've let happen here? It's an absolute disgrace—"

"Now that you've brought Jack back," he said coldly. "You're free to leave."

"Uh-uh! I still have some things I want to say to you."

"I'm really not interested in what you have to say. And please don't come in here, from your polished plastic world, and tell me how I should live. You're not even on the same planet. Now why don't you tell me what's really bothering you, Ms. Maxwell. I think there's a lot more to it than a dustball or two!"

"You're right." She set her hands on her hips, and gave him a look that would have annihilated a lesser man. "I want you to know that Felicity happened to overhear you and Jordan talking the other day, and she told me about your conversation because she felt that as Alice's sister, I had the right to know what you were planning to do—"

"I'm sure Felicity acted with the best of intentions, but she was wrong. The decision was mine alone to make, and—"

"But you went to *Jordan* for advice," Lacey snapped. "You left me out!"

"I went to Jordan because I needed to talk to someone about what I was going to do. I didn't go to him for advice. I went to him for support. I knew what I had to do, it wasn't as if I had any other option. I needed to hear him say it was okay."

"But there could have been another option." Her breasts rose and fell under her silk shirt, as she took in a deep breath, let it out again. "Surrogacy."

"It's out of the question." The harshness in his tone surprised even himself. "I won't consider it."

"That's what Jordan said."

"Then Jordan got it right."

Her eyes burned with challenge. "If you really wanted this baby to be born, you'd surely consider every possible avenue—"

"Not that one, because—"

"I know your reasons. Jordan told me. Having a baby is a family affair, and outsiders shouldn't be involved."

Silence shimmered between them, and he suddenly realized he was standing there in nothing but a towel—not that it seemed to faze her. Of course, she was probably used to seeing men half-naked. Or totally naked. In the world she inhabited nudity was probably run-of-the-mill.

She walked away from him and crossed to the window.

The silence between them continued, but he sensed a buildup of tension in her that made him wary.

"What is it?" he asked. "What are you thinking?"

In a voice that was no longer challenging but quiet, she said, "I was just thinking how happy Alice was here. How happy she was, with you and with Jack. And...how very much she wanted this baby."

What could he say to that? Nothing...even if his throat hadn't tightened with emotion, because what she said was true.

Without turning, she went on, "After our mother died—and you probably know this—I was sent to live with an aunt—a rigid and unloving person—and I was miserable. But after a few weeks, Alice came for me. She'd dropped out of university in order to come back home and bring me up. I owe her, Dermid. And I was never able to repay her."

Now she turned, and he saw that her face was very pale.

"You told Jordan," she said, "that you could never consider surrogacy because having babies was a family matter. I'm family, Dermid."

He looked at her blankly, and then his eyes narrowed. "What the *devil* are you trying to say?"

"This will be my last—my last and *only* chance, to do something to repay my sister for what she did for me. Let *me* be the gestational carrier for your baby, Dermid. For you...and for Alice."

CHAPTER FOUR

"YOU'RE out of your mind!"

Was she? Parked in the ferry lineup half an hour later, Lacey could still hardly believe she'd made the offer. And recalling the incredulous expression on Dermid's face, she knew he'd felt exactly the same. But then he'd started to laugh, harshly, and that had let her know, more than anything else could, just how unworthy he thought her to bear Alice's baby.

Without another word, she'd spun on her heel and walked out. Back to her car. Back to the ferry terminal.

Now, as she waited for the next ferry, she gripped the steering wheel, stared blindly into space, and let her anger come to a full boil. So she wasn't Alice, would never be as wonderful as Alice had been, but she wasn't chopped liver either. Her brother-in-law's response to her offer had been cruel. If he really had wanted this baby as much as he purported to, he'd have jumped at her offer. She was family. She was healthy. And most important of all, she was willing.

Yes, she told herself, she *was* willing. She would do anything for Alice. She would even have put her career on hold. It would be a sacrifice, but nothing compared to the huge sacrifice Alice had made when she'd dropped out of university in order to look after her.

Thinking of Alice brought tears to her eyes. Blinking them away furiously, she pulled herself together.

She had made the offer. McTaggart had refused it.

There was nothing more she could do.

Vancouver Airport was bustling with activity when Dermid arrived. And he was late. Later than he'd planned. Or perhaps, he reflected as he approached the departure lounge, it was because he'd subconsciously hoped to miss his flight.

But that would only have delayed the inevitable.

The plane was already boarding; within minutes he was strapping himself into his aisle seat. And once settled in, he felt suddenly impatient to be on his way. Impatient to do what he had to do and then put it behind him.

He had no option.

His sister-in-law thought he had.

And what she had suggested had to be the most ludicrous thing he'd ever heard. Lacey Maxwell had proved to him, by her impulsive offer, to be just the kind of birdbrain he'd always believed her to be. She hadn't a clue what she'd have been letting herself in for; she hadn't a clue what it meant to carry a baby for nine months.

She'd made the offer as lightly as she'd have suggested making him a cup of tea.

The woman was a flake.

She was also, whispered a little voice in his head, family. Not only that, Alice had loved her and had been incredibly proud of her. And if anyone were to be a suitable surrogate, it would surely be Alice's sister.

But no, it was ridiculous. She might have made the offer, but she'd never have followed through with it. Her looks were her livelihood, and after a pregnancy a woman's body was never quite the same. She hadn't taken time to think of that. But by now she would have, and she'd be thanking her lucky stars that he'd slapped her down—

A small object came flying through the air and rolled onto his knee. Catching it, he saw it was a rattle.

"Sorry!" A female voice came from across the aisle.

He glanced over and saw a pretty young woman with a baby in her arms. A girl baby, dressed in pink.

"Thanks," the woman said as he handed over the rattle. She added, with a twinkling smile, "Her daddy's a pitcher, Leila seems determined to follow in his footsteps."

The baby was blond like her mother, and just as pretty. If Alice had been here, she'd have gone all mushy. He could almost hear her. She would have said, "Isn't she adorable!" And she might have confided, "My husband and I are going to have a baby girl, too, one day!"

He felt as if his heart was being squeezed of blood.

He wanted to say, "She's beautiful. She really is a beautiful baby. You and your husband are very fortunate."

But this throat was thick with emotion, and he couldn't get the words out.

* * *

"Did you have a good workout, Ms. Maxwell?"

"The best, Norm." Lacey paused to chat to the doorman as she entered the foyer of her West Vancouver waterfront condo building. "The gym was quiet, I did my circuit in record time!"

Lacey headed for the elevators and rode up to the tenth floor. On the south-west corner of the building, her condo commanded a spectacular view over the harbour and across the Georgia Strait to Vancouver Island.

But when she walked into her sitting room, what attracted her attention wasn't the view but the pages of printed matter that had spewed from her fax machine, on the phone table, while she was out.

The fax turned out to be from Otto Toeniss, her agent. It consisted of a letter from him along with a several-pages-long contract. And when Lacey read Otto's letter, she thought her heart would burst, as he was writing to tell her that Kinga Koss *was* retiring at the end of the year, and GloryB were interested in having Lacey replace her as their GloryB Girl!

Her heart didn't burst but it did start to sing. She danced around with the contract in her hand until she was giddy, and then, totally out of breath, she set the fax on the coffee table, and headed for the bathroom.

She was eager to read the terms of the contract but she would take her time, savour the experience. First, she'd have her shower, and get dressed, and make coffee.

And then she'd take the papers out to the veranda,

and sit in the glorious sunshine while she read over the words that would make her dreams come true and reward her richly for her many years of hard work and dedication.

Dermid got out of his car and slamming the door, scanned Lacey's luxurious condo building with its sleek lines, sun-sparkled windows, and verandahs adorned with plants.

He was crazy.

He must be…or why else was he here?

He jammed his hands into the pockets of his chinos. Took them out again, and ran a knuckle over his bristled jaw. He must look like an outlaw. He'd been traveling half the night, having turned around in Toronto and caught the next plane back. It was the baby, of course, that had done it. The baby on the plane. The baby in pink. Without knowing it, she had driven him to listen to his heart, and his heart had told him that what he was doing was wrong. It wasn't what *Alice* would have wanted.

So here he was, about to take Lacey Maxwell up on her offer. Provided, of course, that her offer still stood. She might well have changed her mind since yesterday, and would be a fool if she hadn't. From a career point of view. But there was a chance she might stick with her offer. And it was a chance he couldn't turn down.

So here he was. And he'd better get on with it.

He strode to the front door but when he looked at

the panel of suite numbers, he saw no names. Just numbers.

He looked through the plate glass doors and saw a doorman sitting at a desk. He buzzed, and the doorman came over and opened the door.

"I'm here to see my sister-in-law," Dermid said. "Lacey Maxwell. What's her number?"

"We don't give out numbers. If you let me have your name, I'll call her."

Dermid followed him to the desk. "Dermid McTaggart."

The doorman picked up the phone, punched in a number. A moment later, he said, "Ms. Maxwell, I have your brother-in-law here. Dermid McTaggart." After a pause, he said, "Okay, will do. Hang on."

Dermid raised his eyebrows. "What is it?"

"Ms. Maxwell says her brother-in-law is in Toronto—"

"Let me talk to her." He took the phone from the doorman. "Lacey, I'm back. I need to talk to you."

He counted seven beats of his heart before she said, "Put Norm back on the line."

He returned the phone to the doorman, who listened for a few moments, before putting down the phone.

"You're to go up," he said. "Tenth floor. Number's 1002. Elevator's along there, to the left."

The corridor in the tenth floor was carpeted in dark gray, the walls were oyster-white, her door was burgundy.

He pressed the buzzer and stood back.

It was early, he'd probably disturbed her sleep. She'd be in her robe, with her hair all mussed, her eyes bleary—

The door opened and there she was, not disheveled at all but looking stunning in a black T-shirt, heavy pewter chain and immaculately pressed white jeans. Her hair was smooth as black rain, her green eyes clear…but icy-cold.

"Come in." She stood back and gestured to him to enter. Her nail polish was Chinese Red, as was the lipstick on her unsmiling mouth.

The air smelled fresh and breezy, her windows were all open, her furnishings light and modern. Stark. Clinical.

"Would you like a mug of coffee?" she asked.

"This isn't a social call."

"It would have surprised me if you'd said it was." Her tone was only as polite as civility required. "I've just made myself a pot, you won't mind if I have some while you talk?"

She was moving too fast. He'd been in an all-fired hurry to get to her, but now that he was here, he found himself wanting to delay what he'd come to say.

"Since you've already made coffee," he said, somewhat churlishly, "I'll have some."

She left him standing there while she walked into her galley kitchen. When she brought his coffee through, he was about to say "I take sugar," but she beat him to it.

"The sugar's in," she said.

"How did you know I—"

"Because I've seen you often enough, ladling it into your coffee at Deerhaven." She handed him the mug. "I'd even hoped that over time it might sweeten your temperament but my hopes...so far...have been dashed."

He opened his mouth to return with some equally scathing comment, but closed it again. She was hostile enough already, no point in making her worse.

She crossed to her phone table, and pushing aside a sheaf of papers, picked up her coffee mug. "We'll go out to the veranda."

He followed her outside.

"Have a seat," she said.

Instead he walked restlessly over to the railing, and looked out over the water. The ocean was calm, its smoky blue surface brushed with stripes of navy. The only sound to be heard was the roar of an approaching Coast Guard Search and Rescue helicopter, and Dermid waited till it had passed over and the noise had faded to a distant hum before turning around.

Lacey had seated herself on a patio chair, at a table shaded from the sun by a white-and-beige umbrella.

"I'm surprised," she said, "that you're back from Toronto so soon, even allowing for the three-hour time difference. The clinic must open very early in the morning for you to be back here already. So what do you want from me, Dermid? You want my support now that it's *over?*"

"No, it's not—"

"What, then? My blessing? My understanding?" She shook her head and gave a mirthless laugh. "I'm sorry, Dermid, that's not how it works. I'll never understand why you turned down my offer. I'd have thought that you'd have been big enough to put aside your dislike of me and let me carry this baby for you...for Alice's sake and the baby's, if not your own. I hadn't quite realized how worthless a creature you believe me to be."

He had let her run herself out. But now, when she'd finally finished, and he was gearing himself up to explain the purpose of his visit, her phone rang.

"Excuse me." She got up and went inside.

He saw her go to her desk, pick up the phone. She stood with her back to him. Although her voice was slightly muffled, he heard her say,

"Yes, Otto. Yes, it arrived safely. Yes, I'm thrilled. And no, I haven't had time to read it yet. I have company, Otto. Yes, of course I'll call you back."

She came outside again, but didn't sit down. Instead she stood in the open doorway, her hands tucked into the hip pockets of her jeans. If she was "thrilled" over whatever it was that had arrived safely, he certainly couldn't have told it from her eyes.

"I don't think we have anything more to discuss." The sun splashed her hair with molten gold. "And I have some business I must attend to this morning, so—"

"This isn't a social visit. I told you that when I

arrived.'' He set his coffee mug on the railing. ''This is business, too.''

''Go on.''

''When you offered yourself as a surrogate mother, I was very rude—''

''Rude?'' Lacey's snort was scornful. ''You made it clear that even if I were the last woman on earth, I would still not be up to your high standards! So...is that what why you're here? You were *unspeakably* rude and now you want...what? My forgiveness?''

''No.'' The word felt like a lump of lead in his mouth. ''I want to know if your offer still stands.''

Lacey paced the sitting room after he'd gone.

Had she ever felt so mixed-up in her life? Not that she could recall.

When he'd asked if her offer still stood, she'd stared at him for several seconds, too stunned to respond. In the end, she'd stammered, ''B...but haven't you been to the clinic and—''

''I didn't go. Oh, I went to Toronto, but I didn't go to the clinic. I stayed at the airport, caught the first available flight back.''

She'd blinked, bewildered. ''But why?'' she'd asked. ''What changed your mind?''

''That's not important. What I need to know is—''

''What you need to know,'' she said slowly, ''is if I'll have this baby for you. For you, and for Alice.''

''Yes.''

"You've taken me by surprise." She clasped her arms around herself. "I'd put it behind me—"

"Are you saying your answer is no?"

She had stepped off dry land into quicksand...and where was help when it was needed? Not anywhere in sight.

With the GloryB contract within her grasp—a hard fact rather than the thrilling possibility it had seemed just days ago—her decision wasn't going to be an easy one.

She would have to think the matter through. Weigh all the pros and cons. When she'd made the offer, she'd acted impulsively. Yes, she wanted to make a sacrifice to repay Alice for the sacrifices she'd made for her...but when push came to shove, did she have the fortitude to put her career on hold—perhaps damage it beyond repair—by having a baby?

"I guess it's a no." His voice was flat.

"Don't put words in my mouth. It isn't as easy as that, Dermid." *Things have...happened...since last we talked. My situation has changed.* She thought the words, but didn't say them. Instead she said, "Would it be legal? I mean, didn't you and Alice have to sign some kind of a consent form? Isn't there usually a stipulation that on the death of one partner, the embryo be discarded?"

"In our case, because I'm unable to have more children, Alice stipulated that if anything happened to her, any decision about the embryo would be mine to make.'' He shrugged. ''I didn't fight her when she insisted—''

''Because it never occurred to you that she wouldn't be able to have the baby herself.''

''Right.''

''If...and I'm saying if...I agreed to consider having this baby, first you and I would have to sit down and do a lot of talking.''

''So you're not saying no?''

''What I'm saying, Dermid, is maybe.''

''Lacey, it's taken me months to get to this stage, where I'd make my decision. It's not the easiest thing in the world, to—''

''I know. And I won't keep you waiting long. Give me a couple of days. I want to make sure that once I've made my decision I can live with it, because either way, it's going to affect the rest of my life.''

''Till Sunday then? You'll let me know on Sunday?''

''Yes, I'll let you know on Sunday.''

Dermid spent a couple of hours on Sunday morning walking around the perimeter of his property, checking and repairing the chicken wire attached to the outside bottom of the fencing, wire designed to keep out coyotes.

The day was wild, with a fierce wind and gunmetal gray skies. Rain had been forecast for late afternoon, but by the time he'd finished his task, the storm was already sweeping in. Rain lashed down mercilessly, and as he hurried to the house, the deluge soaked him, slapping his shirt to his back and glueing his jeans to his legs.

On occasions such as this, he reflected as he entered the kitchen, Alice would have had a dry towel waiting for him, and soft laughter as she chastised him for not having the sense to come home sooner.

What he got now was an empty house. Arthur had driven up-island to visit his grandfather, taking Jack with him. There was no comfort here, nor would there ever be.

Ripping off his wet shirt, he tossed it into the sink, where it landed on top of the breakfast dishes, which he hadn't got around to washing.

Had she phoned yet?

The question had been buzzing in his head all morning. And without further delay, he went through to his office.

The answering machine was by his computer, but before he reached it, he could see the red light wasn't blinking.

Disappointment smashed into him, but along with the disappointment was anger. She knew how important this was to him, and she must know how stressed he'd be, awaiting her call. Heck, that's why he'd gone out for a couple of hours! He'd been up since dawn, hovering over the phone, but when ten o'clock had rolled around, he couldn't take it any more. So he'd gone out, kept himself busy, while all the time feeling sure a message would be waiting for him when he got back.

Nothing. Nada. Zilch.

And if she hadn't called, the answer must be no.

Stood to reason. If she'd wanted to have this baby, she'd have been eager to let him know. Eager to get on with whatever might have to be done.

She was, as he'd always thought her to be, a useless—

The phone rang.

He froze. Stared at it as if he'd never heard a phone ring before. And then, dragging in a deep breath, he snatched the handset from the cradle, afraid it would stop ringing before he got to it.

"McTaggart here."

"It's me, Dermid. Lacey—"

"It's about time! I've been waiting all bloody morning for your call—"

"I know. I'm sorry. We've had a bit of a wind storm here, and power outages, and the phone lines were down—"

"Okay, okay, I get the picture." He closed his eyes, prayed for patience...and prayed that she had phoned to give him the news he wanted to hear. "So let's cut out the chitchat and get to the point. What's your decision, Lacey? Are you, or are you not, going to stand by your offer?"

CHAPTER FIVE

LACEY'S decision had not been an easy one to make.

She had grappled with the ins and outs of it all day Saturday, and all night, too, for she'd scarcely slept a wink. Then in the early hours of Sunday morning, she'd shawled herself in a fuchsia pashmina and snuggled her feet into thick-knit wool socks, and gone out to the veranda.

She'd sat there, the GloryB contract on the table in front of her, while her head spun from the myriad thoughts and dreams and memories swirling around in her brain.

It wasn't till dawn broke, and she watched its fiery glory streak over the heavens, that she realized she was crying. Tears for her sister, for the baby Alice would never see. Tears for herself, for the contract she would never sign.

But ultimately tears of release, because her decision was made.

Now, as she stood by her desk, with her phone to her ear, she could imagine Dermid standing by his desk, with his phone to his ear, too. He was a south paw, so he'd be holding the receiver with his left hand, and the rich gold of his wedding band would be glinting bright against his tanned skin. Maybe with his right hand, he was plowing back his hair, restlessly, awaiting her decision.

And it wasn't fair to keep him in suspense. It hadn't been her intention. She knew how anxious he must be to hear what she had to say.

And she was just as anxious to say the words out loud, because once spoken, there would be no taking them back.

"Yes," she said. "My offer still stands."

There followed a long moment of silence, then he murmured something. It sounded like "Thank God!"

But when he spoke again, it was in a steady voice.

"So," he said. "That's it."

She sank down onto her chair, her legs wobbly. "What happens now?"

"I phoned the clinic yesterday and explained the situation to the nursing coordinator. She said that if your offer still stood, she'd arrange to have the embryo transferred to their new clinic, here in Vancouver."

"And then...?"

"Then you and I would see our lawyers, have a get-together with them, sort out all the legalities."

"And...?"

"You'd have to go to the clinic, get your health checked out. Then if all was well, the next step would be for you to go on a hormone regime—"

"Hormones? For what purpose?"

"Extra estrogen to make the endometrius nice and thick."

"And how long would this take?"

"It would take about a month to prepare you."

"And after that...?"

"On the morning of the transfer, the embryo would be thawed out ahead of time. Then you'd have it transferred to your uterus. It's a very simple procedure."

Lacey felt oddly breathless. "I see."

"Then it'll be a matter of waiting...for two or three weeks....until you're ready to have a pregnancy test. Any more questions?"

"No." Her voice seemed as insubstantial as she felt! "It seems quite straightforward. So...you'll phone the Toronto clinic tomorrow, set things in motion?"

"First thing in the morning. And tomorrow, call your lawyer, explain what's happening, I'll call mine, we can set up a conference call and get the legal side in order."

"Surely the legalities won't be very complicated?"

"We do have to have a contract. There are things that have to be clearly set out beforehand. For example, I want it in black and white that after this baby is born—if it indeed is born—you relinquish all rights to it."

Lacey's laugh was dry. "That's one thing you can be *absolutely* sure of. You know very well that I don't connect with children till they're out of diapers and able to string a few sentences together! The moment this 'maybe' baby is born I'll hand it over to you, and be more than happy to do so. Infants aren't my thing!"

"Yeah, Alice was the one who loved babies." His

tone had become sober. "Okay, you've made your point on that matter, I agree I have nothing to fear there, but there'll be other matters to discuss. Financial implications—"

"Dermid, *please* don't bring money into this. Having Alice's baby will be—quite literally—a labor of love."

"Fine." He sounded gruff, and she sensed he was getting emotional. And no wonder. He and Alice had wanted this baby so much, and now it was possible that he would, within the year, have their tiny baby daughter in his arms.

"Is that all just now?" Lacey asked. "I should call my agent right away, fill him in on what's happening."

"Yeah, that's it for now. And Lacey..."

"Mmm?"

"Thanks."

Thanks. Such a small word, but coming from Dermid McTaggart, it meant a lot. For a man who hated to be beholden to anyone, it must have been difficult to get out. But he'd managed. And she appreciated it.

"You're very welcome," she said.

"I'll be in touch."

After she'd hung up, Lacey rose from her chair and wandered out to the veranda.

Staring out at the ocean, she felt herself reeling from the magnitude of what she'd just done.

A few weeks from now, if all went well, she was going to be pregnant.

Am I really doing this? she asked herself. Have I really committed myself to having this man's baby for him?

The answer, incredibly, was "Yes!"

"Are you out of your mind?"

Lacey jerked the phone from her ear as her agent's disbelieving voice grated her eardrums. This was the second time in less than a week that a man had asked her the same question. And maybe she was.

She put the receiver to her ear again. "Otto, I know you must think I'm crazy to turn down the chance to be the GloryB Girl, but—"

"And you're not even going to tell me *why?*"

"I can't. At least, not yet. There's something I have to do, but I won't know for maybe a couple of months if it's going to work out. In the meantime, please don't make any new bookings for me. I'm sorry it all sounds so mysterious. All I can say is it's a family project and if things go as hoped it'll be the best part of a year before I'll be available to work again—"

"A *year?*"

Lacey winced. "Yes, I'm afraid so—"

"In a year, my love, you'll be history."

His words, spoken flatly, sent cold shivers down Lacey's spine. And even hours later, when she thought of them, she still felt chilled. Was Otto right? Would it be impossible to resume her career after the baby's birth?

Modeling was her life. And she *loved* that life.

But she had to do this for her family's sake. So, hard as it was, she managed to put her apprehensions behind her.

She contacted her lawyer, May Pickeril, and on Tuesday she went downtown to May's office and they had a long conference call with Dermid and his lawyer.

The discussions went well and a couple of days later, the contract arrived in Lacey's mailbox, and after reading it, she signed it and sent it back.

The following day, Dermid called to tell her he had set up an appointment for her to see a Dr. Martin Cole, at the fertility clinic. She kept the appointment, the doctor found her fit and well, and gave her a prescription for the hormones which she was to take for the next month.

The month passed quickly. Lacey's work took her to New York, and then to Europe, and though her work schedule was hectic, thoughts of the "maybe baby" were never far from her mind.

And she wondered if, for Dermid, it was the same.

Dermid found the time dragging. And although he did his best to concentrate on the day-to-day running of the ranch, he found it impossible to keep his thoughts from wandering to the future. To the possibility that in less than a year from now, he would hold his daughter in his arms.

But whatever lay ahead, he knew the old nightmare would no longer bedevil him. He felt at peace, knowing he had done what Alice would have wanted him to do.

The rest was up to Lacey.

She'd told him she'd be away for most of the month, but that she'd be home the Monday before her appointment at the clinic for the embryo transfer, which was to be on the Wednesday.

When he phoned her on the Monday evening, she said, "Are you checking up on me?"

"No," he said. "I just wanted to touch base. How are you feeling...about Wednesday?"

"Nervous."

"I want to be there."

"I hardly think so!" Her laugh was edgy. "They put women up in stirrups for the procedure—"

"I mean," he said, "that I want to be at the clinic with you, not in the doctor's office."

"Oh. Still, it's not necessary—"

"Not for you, maybe. But it's necessary for me. I want to be part of this, from the very outset." His tone brooked no argument. "Just tell me when you want to leave for the clinic and I'll pick you up."

"It won't work," she said. "I'll have to be out of here by eight. Even if you got the first ferry in the morning, you wouldn't be here in time."

"I'll come over tomorrow night. I'll stay at Deerhaven."

He could sense her reluctance, but she said, "I don't suppose I can stop you, if you're determined to come."

"I am. Lacey, this baby is part of me. How could I not want to be there at such a crucial time?"

After they hung up, he called Deerhaven, and Felicity said she'd be delighted to have him stay over.

"And after you've been to the clinic," she said, "bring Lacey here, we'll have lunch. I know Jordan will want to give his sister a hug and say 'Well done, Lace!'" Felicity sounded awed. "It's so generous, isn't it, what she's doing?"

"Yes," he said. "It's actually beyond generous."

"Lacey's a wonderful person," Felicity said. "Truly one of a kind, Dermid. I know that you and she have never really clicked, but I hope that this—what you're doing—will somehow bring you together so you can be friends."

He and Lacey Maxwell become friends? He doubted that would ever happen. They were poles apart in every way. But while he made a noncommittal response to Felicity's comment, he realized that in view of what Lacey had undertaken to do, he could no longer treat her with the disdain with which he had in the past.

It wouldn't be easy to stop sniping at her; "putting her down" had become an ingrained habit. But in all fairness, he would have to try.

As surrogate mother to his child she deserved no less.

Butterflies cavorted around in Lacey's stomach on Wednesday morning as she emerged from her building—and no wonder, she thought. This was the most momentous day of her life.

Dermid had phoned minutes before, to say he was

on his way down from Deerhaven, and she saw that he had already arrived. His car sat idling in the forecourt. A gray estate car. Solid, reliable, like the man himself.

He was standing beside it, but at sight of her, he walked toward her, swinging along as he always did with the easy confident grace of an athlete.

He was wearing a taupe suit with an oyster-white shirt, and had obviously taken pains with his appearance on this very special day. Lacey was glad she'd chosen to look her best, too, in a slim-fitting pearl-grey dress that she'd bought in Paris just the week before.

Anyone watching them, she reflected, might have thought Dermid was here to take her out on a date...until they noticed the grave expression in his eyes and the unsmiling set of his mouth...and the fact that he greeted her with a cursory nod, rather than a lover's tender kiss!

"Hi," he said. "All set?"

"As all set as I'll ever be!"

"Then let's get this show on the road."

He placed his hand against the small of her back, to steer her to the car. Enclosed in his space, in his earthy male scent, she felt the warmth of his palm through her dress; felt the pressure of his fingertips against her spine—and, to her enormous dismay, she also felt an unexpected and powerful sizzle of sexual electricity.

She wanted to wrench herself from him, but managed to control the automatic reaction. He'd undoubtedly have put such a move down to dislike, and unless she explained the real reason—self-protection!—any hopes of attaining any level of friendliness with him would be dashed.

So instead she smiled pleasantly and thanked him when he opened the passenger door for her. But she was relieved that during the drive to the clinic, he didn't attempt to initiate conversation.

She needed time to sort out her thoughts. And her feelings.

She had always recognized that Dermid was a gorgeous-looking man, but in the past she'd never felt drawn to him, physically or in any other way. On the contrary, the only feelings he'd ever aroused in her had been resentment because of his put-downs. But now, at the most inappropriate of times, she had apparently become susceptible to something she'd never even noticed before: his animal magnetism.

Lord help her!

One thing, though, was in her favor: the man didn't like her. Actually he might even despise her. So even as she acknowledged that if he ever took a notion to seduce her, he already had a head start, she knew she was in no real danger. If there was one man on earth who had no interest in taking her to his bed, it was Dermid McTaggart!

Dermid paced the empty waiting room. Glanced at his watch. Frowned. Glanced at his watch. Paced the room some more.

The doctor had said Lacey would be out in about an

hour, so what was keeping her? Why hadn't she appeared yet? What was—

The waiting room door opened and his sister-in-law came in, a tentative smile hovering around her lips.

"Well?" He scowled at her. "What took you so long?"

She laughed, a shaky laugh. "Oh, Dermid, if you could only see your expression! I'm sorry it seemed long to you, but I've only been in there for a little over an hour. It's over," she said. "Everything went as planned."

"How do you feel?"

"Fine." And then—in what seemed to him an impulsive rush—added, "Odd, actually. Head-spinningly odd!"

Her cheeks were flushed, her eyes a little too bright. Too much excitement, he figured; time for her to relax.

"Let's get ourselves up to Deerhaven, you should put your feet up, take it easy for a while."

"I hope," she said, "that you're not going to start treating me like an invalid!"

"No, but I'm going to make sure you look after yourself properly, and here's how I intend to do it. Lacey, I've already told you I want to be part of this baby's life from the beginning—"

"If there is a baby!"

"Okay, *if* you do become pregnant, I want you to come and live at the ranch, for the duration—"

"No way! I'd go crazy 'way out there in the sticks

for months on end. Besides, I have obligations, I'll be continuing to work until my pregnancy shows—''

A young couple came into the waiting room, and Dermid took her arm and led her to the door. ''Let's leave it just now,'' he said. ''We certainly need to discuss this, but we can do it later, after lunch.''

When they arrived at Deerhaven, Felicity and Jordan had prepared a meal. Jordan greeted his sister with a warm hug, and the ''Well done, Lace!'' which Felicity had predicted.

After the meal, Jordan had to go to work. The baby was asleep, Mandy and her brothers went upstairs for their quiet time, and Felicity brushed aside Lacey's offer to help with the dishes.

''You and Dermid take your coffee out to the deck. I'll join you once I'm finished in here.''

So they went out to the deck, where Lacey sank down on a cushioned lounger, and with a contented sigh, kicked off her pumps and closed her eyes.

Dermid moved over to the railing and looked out over the ocean.

He hadn't expected to feel so off-kilter in the wake of what had happened that morning. Even if the transfer turned out to be successful, Lacey wasn't going to be the mother of his child, she was just a surrogate. Not even a surrogate. Just a carrier. Why, then, did he now feel so entangled with her? Why did he feel this new bond between them—because he *did* feel a bond. The last thing he'd expected—or wanted—was that he would become emotionally involved with her. That could only lead to problems. What they had was a business arrangement, and he wanted it to stay that way.

He'd never thought much of her as a person. He could find no reason to admire a woman who made her living by swanning around in exorbitantly expensive clothes, getting her picture taken. But yet, what she was doing for love of Alice—he shook his head at the magnitude of it—

He heard the rustle of her dress, smelled her musky gardenia scent, two seconds before she appeared at his side.

"A penny for them," she said. "But maybe, today, they're worth much more than that."

She took up a stance with her back to the railing, leaning against it, her elbows resting on the top rail, her lips curved in a faint smile as she regarded him.

Her beauty stole his breath away.

The sun glistened in her black hair, gilded her creamy skin, sparkled in her green cat's eyes.

And as he stared into the clear green depths, he felt as if the deck had swayed under his feet, like the deck of a storm-tossed boat.

He tried to drag his gaze away, but couldn't.

What the heck was happening to him?

"A penny?" he said, trying to sound casual. "No, you're right, they're worth more than a penny today. But I guess I don't need to tell you what I'm thinking, you must be having the same kind of thoughts yourself."

He doubted it! She seemed to be totally at ease standing so close to him, whereas he was struggling against a burning desire to feel that glossy black hair under his fingertips and feel that glossy red mouth under his own—

He desired her.

The realization shook him to the core. Of all the women in all the world, the last one he should want to take to his bed would be Lacey Maxwell.

Dammit, he would have to rethink his plan to have her stay at the ranch. Instead he'd have to settle for monitoring her from a distance.

He'd known she'd fight to keep her independence, but he'd also been sure that with the judicious use of emotional blackmail, he could win her over. *It's what Alice would have wanted,* was what he'd planned to say. And it would have knocked the fight right out of her.

"I was thinking," she murmured, "about what you said at the clinic. I'm sorry I was so obstructive, Dermid. And so selfish. You have every right to be involved with this baby from the beginning, and I'm only sorry that I have some commitments I do have to keep. But by the time I'm four or five months pregnant, I'll be free to move over to the ranch, and I'll stay there till the baby's born—"

"Lacey, I—"

"Dermid, you don't have to thank me. Truly you don't. I'm doing this not only for you—and for Jack."

Her eyes had become misty. "It's what Alice would have wanted."

Ironically, without even being aware of it, she had used his own argument against him. And what could he do about it? Nothing!

Before he could make any response, Felicity came out to join them. And not long after, Lacey said she should be getting home, so he drove her back to her condo.

As he dropped her off, she said, "The nurse at the clinic is going to call and set up a date for the pregnancy test."

"Let me know ahead of time and I'll come over."

She hesitated. "Dermid, would you mind terribly if I do this on my own? I know you want to be as much a part of this whole process as you can, but in this instance, it's just that...if the news isn't good...well, I think both of us would rather be on our own when we found out."

He hesitated, too, before he gave his answer. And then he nodded. "Yeah, I guess you're right. It would be pretty hard to take. So you'll go to the clinic alone...but you'll phone me as soon as you get the test results?"

"Yes," she said, obviously relieved. "Of course."

Dermid finished cleaning up a dung pile in one of the pastures, and taking a break, leaned back against the fence. The afternoon sun was scorching hot and he could feel sweat running down under his shirt and dribbling into the waistband of his jeans.

Gazing out over the rolling fields, he was barely aware of the llamas and alpacas browsing nearby. His mind was miles away. Over on the Mainland.

Three weeks had passed since his visit to the clinic with Lacey; three weeks during which he hadn't heard a single word from her.

He'd phoned her place twice during the past few days, but each time he'd got the answering machine. He'd had to hold onto his patience, but it was fast running out—

"Dad!"

He turned his head and saw Jack racing toward him, with Scamp, the farm dog, at his heels.

But even as he looked questioningly at his son, something by the house caught his attention.

A flash of color.

His gaze flicked past Jack and the dog.

And when he saw what had distracted him, his heartbeats staggered.

Lacey Maxwell, in white pants and a scarlet top, was standing in his courtyard, beside her flashy silver car.

"Dad, Aunt Lacey's here!" Jack wheeled around and chased after Scamp who had taken off after a butterfly.

Valentine, the eleven-month-old female llama Dermid had bought the previous weekend, sauntered up on the other side of the fence and nudged Dermid.

He set a hand on her back, abstractedly running a hand through the coat of fleece, its softness lighter than silk.

Then he dropped his hand and started walking toward Lacey. It seemed to him he was moving in slow motion, it took forever to close the distance between them.

She waited by the car, and it wasn't till he was almost up to her that he saw the smile in her eyes.

The tightness he'd been feeling for days snapped, releasing a surge of joy that was almost too great to bear.

He cleared his throat as emotion clogged it.

"So," he said gruffly. "The news is good?"

"The best it could possibly be!" Her happiness and delight spilled out in a lilting laugh. "Congratulations, Dermid. You're going to have a baby!"

CHAPTER SIX

LACEY and Dermid decided that he would share the news with Arthur, but they agreed he shouldn't tell Jack yet.

"Time enough," Lacey suggested, "when I move over here for the second half of the pregnancy. We can explain everything then."

She stayed just long enough to have a glass of iced tea with Dermid at the picnic table in the backyard.

When she got up to leave, Dermid said, "You're going already? You came all this way just to turn around and—"

"I didn't want to tell you over the phone," Lacey said. "It was too important, too exciting, I simply had to tell you in person." She grinned. "It was worth the trip, just to see the look on your face."

"You looked pretty happy yourself!"

"I am." She swung the strap of her bag over her shoulder as they walked around to the car. "But my agent won't be—although he'll be relieved that I still plan on honoring my commitments for the next four or five months."

"So you'll be back here before the snow flies?"

"And it usually starts to fly in November."

She paused as Dermid opened her car door. "We are doing the right thing, aren't we?"

"It's too late to be having doubts, Lacey."

"Well, yes, I know...but bringing a baby into the world, knowing it won't have a mother—"

"You're worried about that?"

"Aren't you?"

"Alice would have wanted this baby to be born. I believe that so strongly that it overrides any other concern. But although the child won't have a mom, she'll have a very caring family. She'll have Jack and me to love her, and she'll also have Arthur and the Deerhaven folks. And then there'll be you," he teased, "once she's out of diapers and able to string a few words together."

He was taking the whole thing in his stride. And she felt ashamed that she'd been having doubts. Dermid McTaggart was a family man, always had been. And she should have had more confidence in him.

He touched her upper arm, briefly but reassuringly. "It's going to work out, Lacey. Just take very good care of yourself. And let me know if there's anything, anything at all, I can do to help, between now and November."

"I will. I'll probably see you before then, though, if I chance to be around when you visit Deerhaven."

But as it happened, she and Dermid didn't meet up with each other again until November.

Otto had rearranged her schedule, although at her

request he had kept her pregnancy secret. He had, however, mercilessly crammed as many of her contracted shoots as possible into the time available and her life had become a veritable whirlwind. Fortunately she didn't suffer from morning sickness, and if it hadn't been for an extra fullness in her breasts and an increasing need to catnap, she would scarcely have known she was pregnant.

The months skimmed by, and almost before she knew it, it was September, October…

November.

Lacey's final shoot was in New York, and afterward, en route to the airport, she dropped by Otto's office.

"You look washed-out," he said. "I just hope that when this—" he waved a fat beringed hand at her stomach "—is all over, you—and your career—won't be washed up!"

"You've been a dear, Otto. Thanks for everything. And once this—" smiling wryly, she patted her stomach "—is all over, I'll be in touch. Who knows, motherhood may have given me a new bloom!"

He snorted. "A new shape, more like!" But before she left, he enfolded her still-slender figure in his chubby arms. "Good luck, kid." Otto wasn't one to bear a grudge. "Phone me next spring, I'll see what I can do for you."

She was glad to get home from New York.

But she was so exhausted that although it was only four in the afternoon, after phoning Felicity to tell her she was back and inviting her out for lunch next day, she crawled into bed and fell fast asleep.

When she woke up, it was eleven o'clock next morning.

She felt better. Refreshed. And anxious to be up and about.

But not anxious to go to the ranch.

"I'm dreading it," she said to Felicity as they chatted over lunch in one of downtown Vancouver's trendy restaurants. "Can you imagine me, stuck out in the country, with no theater, no symphony, no galleries—no yummy guys to ogle at the gym..." She heaved out a melodramatic sigh. "Heavens, there won't even *be* a gym!"

Felicity chuckled. "You'll have to find someway to amuse yourself. You could take up knitting or petit point or join the local women's institute and do good works."

Lacey's laugh rolled out, an earthy laugh that raised eyebrows at the next table. "Can't you just see me, judging a pie-making contest at a harvest fete when I don't even know how to make pastry? Get real, Fliss!"

"Does Dermid know you can't cook?"

"Oh, yes. But even if he didn't," Lacey added, "he'd assume it. I'm sure that in his own mind he constantly compares me with Alice and finds me sadly lacking. As I am, when it comes to domestic skills."

"So he won't be expecting you to take over and run the household?"

"Heaven forbid!" Lacey shuddered. "And therefore he will be blessed."

"Blessed?"

Lacey's eyes twinkled. "'Blessed is he who expecteth nothing, for he shall not be disappointed.'"

"And you believe Dermid expects nothing from you?"

"All he expects from me is that I take good care of myself for the next few months so that at the end of that time I'll present him with a happy healthy baby." She sat back in her chair, her expression ironic as she looked at her sister-in-law. "What I am to Dermid McTaggart is nothing more nor less than a baby-hatching machine."

"Does he know you're back?"

"I phoned him this morning. Told him I'd just got home and I needed a few days to rest. I said he could expect me at the weekend."

"So you'll go over on Friday?"

"That was the plan. But I may go over earlier." She toyed restlessly with her silver bracelets. "The longer I put it off, the more I'll dread it. In fact—" she exhaled a sigh "—I think I'll go over tomorrow."

"You'll let him know you're coming?"

"No." Lacey reached for the check as the waitress set it on the table. "I think I'll surprise him!"

Lacey caught the ten-thirty ferry next morning and arrived at the ranch a couple of hours later.

The day was sunny but cool, the November sky a

hard blue. The air was country-fresh and tinged with the scent of wood smoke drifting over from a neighbouring farm.

Lacey parked close to the back door and sat for a few moments listening to the silence. Absolute silence.

She found it unsettling. She wasn't used to such stillness. It gave her the creeps.

"Hi!"

She almost jumped out of her skin as she heard Dermid's voice. Swiveling in her seat, she saw him standing by the main barn, about twenty feet away, his hands planted on his hips.

She glowered at him. "You shouldn't do that!"

"Do what?"

He was wearing a sweat-stained shirt, and his hair had bits of hay in it, and he looked earthy and rugged and a hundred per cent male. Lacey was irritated that she found his craggy wind-beaten features so attractive, and she took the irritation out on him. "Sneak up on people. You could give somebody a heart attack!"

He gestured at the distance between them. "I wouldn't call this exactly 'sneaking up.'"

"Oh, you know what I mean." She jerked open her car door, and getting out, slammed it shut.

"You're early." His tone was mild.

"Is that a problem?" she challenged.

He lifted one broad shoulder in a casual shrug. "Not for me. Although, if I'd known you'd be here today I'd have got your room ready for you."

She unlocked the trunk of her car and was about to heft out her case, but he got there before her.

"Allow me," he said, hoisting the case out.

"I'm quite capable of—"

"I'm sure you are." He closed the trunk. "But while you're pregnant with my child, I don't want you doing any heavy lifting. Okay?" Case in hand, he looked at her, his manner friendly, his eyes questioning.

She was ashamed of herself for having snarled at him. What a bad start—

"Lacey, I know this is difficult for you. It's difficult for me, too. But we'll get through it better if we try to be amicable." He frowned. "You're looking tired. Dammit, I wish you could have been here the last few months, instead of racing around the world, busy busy busy. I phoned you several times, all I got was the answering machine. Seems you were never home."

"But Felicity gave you updates, didn't she?"

"Oh, sure. At least I knew you hadn't fallen off the face of the earth." He swung the case toward the house. "Let's get you inside. It's not good for you to be standing around."

Once inside, he led her to the stairs.

"You might as well get settled in," he said. "And while you're unpacking, I'll hunt up some sheets. Arthur's going to be using my en suite bathroom while you're here, you'll be sharing the main one with Jack. Do you mind?"

"Of course not."

"If you did, Jack could use my en suite, too—"

"Dermid, I'm going to be here for months. Let's stick to your usual routine as much as possible. I really don't mind sharing with Jack."

"Fine."

"Where *is* he? Out with Arthur?"

"No, he's taken Scamp for a romp. Arthur's gone up-island. His grandfather died on the weekend, and Arthur had to arrange the funeral. He should be back any day."

Dermid's bedroom was to the left of the landing, along with a small nursery and Arthur's room; Jack's bedroom and the main bathroom and the guest room were to the right.

Dermid opened the guest room door and stood back to let Lacey enter first. He'd just walked over to the bed and set her case beside it when the phone rang downstairs.

"Excuse me," he said. "I'd better get that."

Without waiting for a response, he took off, leaving Lacey alone.

She'd slept here several times in the past, and Alice had always prepared the room for her. There had invariably been fresh linen on the bed; a vase on the bedside table with a sweet nosegay of flowers; a pile of magazines and paperback books; and even a chocolate mint on the pillow.

Alice had been a perfect hostess.

Lacey grimaced as she surveyed the bedroom now. The air was stale, the furniture dusty, the carpet hadn't been vacuumed for months. And had a bed ever looked less inviting? Looking at it, with its bare mattress and its four pillows with their striped navy and white ticking covers, she felt an almost overwhelming urge to "check out" and go to the nearest Holiday Inn!

However—she dumped her leather shoulder bag on the bed—a deal was a deal. She'd promised Dermid she'd stay here until his baby was ready to be born and stay here she would.

She crossed to the window, and opening it, took in a deep breath of the crisp November air as it seeped in—

"Right, we're in business."

She turned, and saw Dermid coming in, with sheets.

He tossed them onto the dresser, disturbing a cloud of dust. Opening the closet, he pulled a floral duvet down from the shelf, and a white quilted mattress pad. Dropping them on the mattress, he said, "You can make your bed up later. Why don't you just unpack and then come down. I'll put on the coffeepot."

"I've gone off coffee. But a cup of tea would hit the spot."

"Tea. Sure."

He was gone again, as if he couldn't wait to be out of her presence. He had certainly appeared very friendly and helpful since her arrival, but had it been a facade? And under that facade, did he still dislike her so much he couldn't bear to be in the same room with her?

Mulling this over, she crossed the passage to the bathroom to wash her hands.

And stopped short in the doorway.

Wet towels lay clumped on the floor, water puddled the countertop, an empty toilet roll lay in one of the two sinks, and bone-dry soap and an equally dry face-cloth gave ample evidence as to how little her nephew or his father cared about his state of cleanliness.

She picked her way over the towels, and gave a little shriek when a plate-size spider scuttled over her sandal. Shuddering, she made a hasty retreat, and shuddering again, she hurried back to the bedroom.

She hadn't expected the house to be the way Alice had kept it, but she had expected that Dermid would have cleaned it up for her arrival. He couldn't expect her to live like this. Something had to be done about it.

Straightening her spine, she marched out of the bedroom again, and made her way down to the kitchen.

The kettle was singing.

The kitchen was empty.

She crossed to the back door, which was open.

And she saw Dermid outside. He was standing just a few yards away, beside Alice's garden—at least what had once been Alice's garden, but was now just a wild tangle of weeds and overgrown shrubs and dead plants.

She opened her mouth to call to him, but slowly closed it again when she noticed how helpless he looked. Helpless, solitary, lost. She heard him give a weary sigh. Saw him drag a hand through his hair.

And she felt her heart go out to him.

She could well imagine what he must be thinking to

cause such an air of desolation: "If only Alice were here. If only it were *Alice* carrying our baby. If only... if only..."

Tears pricking her eyes, Lacey swallowed hard and withdrew into the house.

It must be painful for him, having her in his home. And she wasn't about to add to his distress by being a burden to him. An irritation.

The kettle started to whistle, she heard his steps coming toward the kitchen door.

Quick as a flickering shadow, she darted from the kitchen and made her way back to her room, not wanting him to know she had witnessed him at such a very low moment.

When she went downstairs again five minutes later, she found Dermid in the kitchen. Outside, not too far away Jack was yelling, "Hey, Scamp, c'mon, fetch me that stick!"

She asked Dermid, "Have you told Jack about the baby?"

He looked up from the packet of cookies he was opening. "You and I agreed not to—"

"I know. I was just wondering..."

"I'll tell him when the right moment presents itself." He poured her tea into a heavy ceramic mug. "Do you take anything in this?"

"Just lemon." She opened the fridge door and flinched. The interior of her own fridge was always sparkling clean and the contents neatly arranged. Here, not only was there enough cholesterol to feed an army, everything—from slabs of cheese to cartons of eggs to jugs of full fat milk to packaged meats—was so jammed together it was a wonder the fridge didn't groan in protest.

And never a lemon in sight.

Nor any other thing that belonged in the fruit and vegetable section of the *Canada Food Guide.*

"Where do you keep your fruit and veg?" she asked.

"We've run out." He poured himself a glass of water. "The mall's a couple of miles along the highway—just keep your receipts and we'll settle at the end of each month."

She sank down on one of the chairs and carefully set her hands on the table in front of her. "You want me to do the shopping? You and I never did discuss the housekeeping arrangements here. Just what do you expect of me?"

"Initially, I hadn't expected anything. I hadn't thought that far ahead. But I guess what I basically expect from you is that you'll eat properly, keep good hours, have lots of walks and fresh country air—"

"I know I have to look after my health, and you won't get any argument from me there. But we never talked about how I'd fill in my day."

"I guess I just expected you'd fit in the way you did on the odd occasion when you came to visit Alice. You just...lounged around..."

"Back then, Alice did all the housekeeping and it was very pleasant just 'lounging around'! But now the place is a mess. Good grief, if you don't have time to keep it clean, you should get a cleaning company in—''

''No way. I can't abide having strangers poking their noses in where they don't belong. Besides,'' Dermid took a swig of water from his glass, ''this is an easy house to run. Alice always said so. Heck, she managed to do it with one hand behind her back and a baby to look after—not to mention spinning the wool and running her own business selling the alpaca sweaters she knitted.''

''I'm not Alice, I'm me. And scrubbing floors isn't my 'thing.'''

''No,'' he returned, with a lazy smile. ''Posing for pictures is your 'thing.' But hey, if you don't want to do any housework, if you're afraid of getting your nail polish chipped, that's okay. I can live with a little dust—''

''And what about meals?''

''When it comes to meals, you'll eat properly, I won't budge on that. Three squares a day. You're welcome to make your own. But if I don't like the look of what you're eating, you'll eat whatever I dish up for myself and Jack and Arthur.''

''Which would be?''

''Burgers, pizzas, corned beef hash, frozen lasagna—''

She gave a delicate shudder. And took a sip of her tea.

This was *tea?* Tar couldn't have tasted worse!

Shoving the mug to one side, she got to her feet. "I'm going out to get some groceries. I'd appreciate it if you could clear a space for me in that cholesterol-laden fridge before I get back. Oh, and while I'm out," she added facetiously, "is there anything I can get for you? A pound of lard, a tub of ice cream, a chocolate cheesecake?"

"Forget about the lard, but the ice cream and chocolate cheesecake sound great. If you'll pick some up, we can have that for dessert tonight after our burgers."

As she headed for her room to get her purse, Lacey rolled her eyes. Ice cream and chocolate cheesecake indeed. The man actually thought she'd been serious!

"When's Aunt Lacey going to get back, Dad?"

Dermid liked to barbecue year-round, and depending on the weather, he and Arthur and Jack ate either outside at the picnic table, or indoors in the kitchen. Today, because the wind had dropped, and the sun gave this sheltered corner of the patio some warmth, he and Jack would eat outside.

Now, as he flipped over the burgers on the grill, he replied to his son's question. "Who knows?"

He wished *he* knew! Arthur's weekly trips to the mall took him about thirty minutes; Lacey had been gone for more than two hours. And he didn't like it. She was carrying his baby, he wanted to know what she was doing every minute of every day.

"Are the burgers almost ready, Dad?"

"Yup. Could you bring out the buns?"

"Sure."

Cosily dressed in his red parka and jeans and boots, Jack clumped away to the patio doors, and Dermid watched as he slid open the door and went in.

He loved the boy so much it sometimes hurt.

And before the year was out, he'd have a little girl, too, to love. Maybe she'd have golden hair like her mother, maybe she'd have a heart-shaped face like her mother, and maybe she'd even have Alice's freckled nose, her three-cornered smile...

He hoped to God she would, because it was almost three years now and with every day that passed he was losing the once crystal-clear memory of his wife's face and he needed to get it back. But no matter how he tried to retain it in its former clarity, it was fading, creating an *emptiness* in him. An aching feeling of loss.

And what was worse than the feeling of loss was the soul-deep feeling of guilt, because *other* images were creeping in now to take their place.

Images of her sister.

A dark frown clouded his brow. He didn't want this to happen. He didn't want to feel attracted to—

"Dad, you're going to burn the burgers!"

He turned his attention to the barbecue, and rescuing the burgers before they became charred, transferred them to a plate. "Thanks, Jack, got 'em just in time."

"Aunt Lacey's back—when I was in the kitchen I saw the car coming up the driveway."

Scamp must have heard the vehicle because he got

up from under the cedar picnic table, and barked sharply.

"I'll go around and help her bring in the groceries," Dermid said. "How about you put the burgers together?"

"One for Aunt Lacey, too?"

"I doubt she'll eat one. But just in case..."

"What should I put on it?"

"Same as ours. Give her the works.'

Dermid went around the side of the house and was in time to see Lacey open the trunk of her car. She was wearing the same black pantsuit and white shirt she'd been wearing when she arrived earlier, and as she leaned over to pick up grocery bags, her hair parted at the nape and slid forward like two skeins of black satin. He'd never seen such fabulous hair anywhere...nor such a sexy rear-end, nor such long, long legs—

Annoyed with himself for being so easily distracted by her appearance, he said, "You *took* long enough!"

"I was delayed." Her voice was muffled. Grasping two of the bags she straightened and turned around.

And when he saw her face, he felt as if one of his alpacas had stomped him in the stomach. Her cheeks were pale, her left cheek was grazed, her upper lip swollen. And scarlet spots—*could that be blood?*—spattered the collar of her formerly pristine white shirt.

"What the *devil,*" he asked grimly, "have you been up to?"

CHAPTER SEVEN

LACEY already felt close to tears. It didn't help that Dermid's eyes flashed with anger and his jaw was clenched.

Without giving her time to answer, he snapped "Put down those bags." Swooping the grocery bags from her, he dropped them back into the trunk alongside the other three. "Let's get you inside!"

With his arm at her back he propelled her into the kitchen and sat her down.

"Now tell me," he said, "exactly what happened!"

"I had an accident in the parking lot at the mall. I...tripped...and fell, on my way to the car."

"You'll have to see a doctor."

"I went into the medical clinic at the mall. The doc cleaned up my face, said it should heal nicely." And since her face was her fortune that had been an enormous relief. But her primary concern had been with the baby. Before she could say so to Dermid, however, he snapped,

"And the baby?"

"The baby's going to be fine too. It wasn't a bad fall, Dermid—it's not as if I'd tumbled down a flight of stairs—"

"You look as shaken as if you had! How could you be so bloody careless!"

If he'd been kind to her, the tears might have fallen. And if the tears had fallen, she might have broken down and told him what had really happened at the mall. She might have told him about the toddler who had shot out of nowhere into the path of a truck and if she hadn't been there, if she hadn't leaped after him when she did—

She stood. "I'm going upstairs to change."

He said, "I'll make you a cup of tea." And turned his back on her, hostility zinging out at her like invisible arrows.

What an unrelenting oaf he was. Tea he was willing to provide, but forget about sympathy. The word wasn't in the man's vocabulary.

The kitchen window was open; she could smell the tantalizing aroma of barbecuing burgers. It made her mouth water. She hadn't realized how hungry she was. She'd planned on making a salad for her dinner, but—

"Dad!" Jack's voice sailed in through the window. "When are you coming out for your burger?"

"In a minute. I'm going to take the groceries in first, and put them away."

As Lacey walked along to the foyer, she heard the phone ring. After a couple of rings, Dermid picked it up.

"McTaggart here," he said.

And then, running up the stairs, she heard no more.

She changed into a cashmere turtleneck sweater and

wool slacks; and after putting her white shirt to soak in cold water in the bathroom sink, she went downstairs.

As she padded along the passage to the kitchen, she heard no sounds from up ahead, and wondered if Dermid had gone outside, but when she reached the doorway she saw he was still there. He'd brought in the groceries but hadn't yet put them away; the bags were on the kitchen table.

And Dermid was standing with his back to her, at the far end of the kitchen. He was looking at a framed photo on the wall. A photo of Alice.

Lacey felt as if she was intruding. But as she hesitated, he must have sensed her presence for he turned.

The expression in his eyes was stark.

"I'm not doing very well, am I!" he said.

She realized, with a jolt, that *he* was the one who needed sympathy. And she was more than prepared to give it to him.

"Dermid—" she took a few steps toward him "—it's going to take time. It's been less than three years...and actually we all think you're doing just great. You could so easily have become a hermit out here, but you've always made an effort to keep in touch with the family—"

"I'm not talking about Alice. I'm talking about you. About the way I am with you. All I ever do is find fault with you—"

"Dermid—"

"A man called Alan Naslund phoned just now.

Apparently you saved his son's life today when his wife and the child were at the mall, and he wanted you to know how grateful he is.''

''Is the little boy all right?''

''Right as rain.'' Dermid made an appealing gesture with his hands. ''Lacey, why didn't you *tell* me?''

Lacey felt the sting of tears, and as they welled up, she ripped a paper towel from a roll on the wall, and with an embarrassed grimace, dabbed her eyes. ''Because,'' she said, ''I knew that if you offered me a kind word, *this* would happen!''

''I've never seen you cry before—but then I've never been kind to you before. What an indictment that is!''

He looked so helpless, so ashamed, she wanted to put her arms around him, tell him it was all right. Instead she just said, ''Alice would hate for us to be fighting. Does it have to be this way, Dermid? I know you don't like me, you've never liked me, but—''

''Lacey, I—''

''C'mon, Dad!'' Jack's voice shrilled in from the patio. ''Tell Aunt Lacey her burger's *ready!*''

Dermid closed his eyes briefly, opened them again. Exhaling a sigh, he said, ''We made enough that you can have one, Lacey, if you want it. Jack and I are going to eat on the patio, but you may find it too cool out there.''

Lacey didn't want to talk about burgers or patios or how cool it was outside. She wanted to hear whatever it was he'd been about to say before Jack had interrupted. But the moment had been shattered.

"I'd like to try one of your burgers," she said. "And I don't mind eating outside. I'll just go up and get a warm jacket—"

"Here, take one of mine." He crossed to the row of hooks by the back door, and took down a quilted green parka. He held it out and she walked over to take it.

He helped her on with it, and as she zipped it up, he said, "Lacey, I don't dislike you." When she looked up at him, startled, he added, "How could I? I don't even know you!"

Because you've never let yourself know me, she wanted to cry, but couldn't. The intense expression in his eyes, along with the disturbing closeness of his solid male body was making it difficult for her to draw breath.

"You were lucky," he murmured, his gaze dropping to her mouth, lingering there, "that you didn't split that lip and need stitches. And your cheek, it's only very lightly grazed, it should be fine in a—"

"Dad!" Jack burst into the kitchen. "When—ooh!, what happened to your *face,* Aunt Lacey?"

Lacey felt, for a frozen moment, as if she and Dermid were in a tableau, neither breathing nor moving, and then the moment melted away, and Dermid dropped his hand.

"Your aunt," he said, "saved a little boy's life today."

He went on to tell Jack the story, and when he'd finished, Jack said,

"Wow, Aunt Lacey, you're a hero! But does your face hurt?"

"A bit."

"Dad'll kiss it better. He's really good at that. Go on, Dad."

Feeling awkward and ready to laugh off the suggestion, Lacey was taken aback when Dermid said, "Why not?"

He clasped her shoulders and lowering his head, he touched his mouth gently to her grazed cheek...and then...he brushed his mouth—very tenderly—over her swollen upper lip.

It was something between a caress and a kiss. But it lasted longer than it should have. She felt the hard strength of his fingers as they grasped her more tightly.

"Okay," Jack said. "Let's have those burgers now!"

Dermid drew back. He looked dazed—as if he'd bitten into a chocolate, Lacey thought, and found a center he hadn't expected. Coffee instead of coconut? Peppermint rather than cherry?

She couldn't tell from his face if the taste and flavor of the experience had been pleasant, or not.

For her, it had been sweeter than any chocolate. And it had made her knees weak.

Somehow she managed an amused smile. "Thanks," she said. "I feel better already!"

And wanting to get away before Dermid saw the hot

blush rising to her cheeks, she let Jack grab her hand and pull her out to the patio.

Kissing her had been a mistake.

The atmosphere between them had always been brittle; now the brittleness had taken on a dangerous quality. He felt as if he was walking on glass and if he put a foot wrong the glass would shatter and he'd tumble into space.

Did she feel the same?

He doubted it. She'd acted as if the kiss had merely amused her. And as far as kisses went, with her experience it probably didn't even rate! She moved in glamorous circles and had no doubt been kissed by the kind of men who routinely set the scene for romance with wine and violins and gourmet dinners at the world's best restaurants.

Well, he himself was certainly not out to "romance" his sister-in-law. The last thing he wanted was to become involved in that kind of a relationship with her. But he couldn't deny that having her around had wakened feelings of desire that had lain dormant for the past three years.

The long period of celibacy had left him vulnerable, he told himself. That's all it was. What he had to do was focus his mind on other things...such as putting away the groceries.

So he put them away, and then he went outside, determined to ignore her, in the way he'd ignore a perfectly sculpted mannequin propped up in a chair.

But when he saw her, he couldn't take his eyes away from her. Far from sitting stiffly as a mannequin, she was leaning over the picnic table and digging into her burger, savoring it with a keenness that astonished him.

Rolling her eyes, she mumbled, "Oh, Dermid, this is delicious!"

"Jordan always swears you exist on lettuce leaves," he said. "With the occasional slice of tomato thrown in!"

She grinned—a mischievous twinkle of green eyes, a sparkling glint of white teeth. "Jordan likes to poke fun at me." She licked a morsel of relish from her thumb. "I do, of course, have to watch what I eat, it's part and parcel of my job. But on occasion I allow myself to fall off the wagon. And only when I think it's going to be worth it. Your burgers—" she took another bite with the gusto of a starving teenager "—are worth it!"

Jack and Arthur always scarfed down his burgers, but never once had either of them said, "Hey, these are good!" Lacey's compliment made him feel oddly warmed.

She offered to serve their dessert, and when she came back outside with it, he found his gaze glued to her as she moved around the patio, serving chocolate cake and ice cream first to Jack, who was on the swing set...

And now to him.

He'd been leaning against the wooden railing at the

far end of the patio, but he straightened as he took the plate from her. "Thanks," he said.

"You're welcome."

"You're not having any?"

She paused, and slid her hands into the pockets of his jacket. "No, I've more than used up my calorie allowance for the day. Maybe tomorrow."

"You'll be putting on weight soon, whether you like it or not."

"That'll be different."

He dug his dessert fork into the cake, held out a morsel to her. "Want to try some?"

"No, when it comes to chocolate, I'm an 'all-or-nothing' gal!"

He forked it into his own mouth. He thought she might move away, but instead, she leaned against the railing, with her back to it. "How quiet it is here."

"You miss the city?"

"It's in my blood. It excites me—the busyness of it during the day, the lights at night..." She glanced around, at the pastures to one side, the trees arcing the house at the other. "I feel...restless here. As if I want something but don't quite know what it is. This—" she waved a hand out vaguely "—just isn't my scene."

"Have you any regrets about...?" He nodded toward her stomach.

"No. Once I'd made up my mind to go ahead, that was it. I'm prepared to put my own life on hold for as long as it takes." She raised her gaze to follow the flight of an eagle as it glided over the nearby trees. "Alice would have done the same for me."

"Yeah. That she would."

Jack had finished his dessert. He crossed to the table and put down his plate. "Dad, when you're ready, we should go and check on Sunflower."

Sunflower, a golden-brown llama, was expected to go into labor at any time.

"Right, son." Dermid finished his dessert, too, and set his plate on top of Jack's. "Let's go."

As Jack ran off, with Scamp at his heels, Dermid turned to Lacey.

"The rule here is that whoever cooks doesn't do the cleanup. Are you okay with that?"

Her gaze flickered over the picnic table with its pile of dirty dishes. He thought he detected a faint shudder. But all she said was, "That sounds fair."

"Don't bother with the grill. That's my job."

He strode off after Jack…but found himself wishing he could have stayed. And he found that disconcerting. Usually, when one of his animals was close to birthing, that became his top priority, and his mind became focused on the safe delivery of the new cria.

But even when he caught up with Jack, and they discovered that Sunflower had indeed gone into labor, thoughts of Lacey weren't so easily displaced.

It wasn't till the birth started to go wrong that finally he forgot all about his sister-in-law.

From the phone in the barn, he placed a call to the vet, and then sent Jack up to the house.

* * *

"Dad doesn't let me hang around when there's a problem," Jack said to Lacey. "He says I'm not old enough. But he always lets me come back right after the cria's born, so's I can see it learn to stand and walk. Have you ever seen a newborn cria, Aunt Lacey?"

"No." Lacey wrapped the left-over chocolate cake in Clingfilm and stored it in the fridge. "I haven't."

"They're *awesome.*" Jack stood at the kitchen window, looking out over the driveway. "And—oh, here's Abigail!"

"Who's Abigail?"

"The vet. Come see."

Lacey crossed to the window and was in time to see a well-built young woman, with flame-red hair, striding toward the barn, bag in hand. Dressed in jeans and a plaid shirt, she looked right at home in the rustic setting.

"I think," Jack said, "that Abby likes my dad. I know he likes her. He might even marry her. I heard him say to Arthur once that she'd make a top-notch rancher's wife."

The woman had disappeared into the barn, and Lacey hadn't had a chance to see her face. But before she could wonder about that, Jack added, "And Arthur said that she sure was the prettiest vet *he'd* ever seen!"

It had never occurred to Lacey that Dermid might have a woman in his life. But he was, after all, a red-blooded male and would have needs the same as any other man.

Still, it came as a shock to her that he might be involved with someone. She'd pictured him grieving for Alice indefinitely.

But if this woman was going to be the next Mrs. Dermid McTaggart, she would not only be Jack's step-mother, she would also be "Mom" to this baby Lacey was carrying now.

And Lacey found that disturbing.

In an effort to take her mind off it, she concentrated on getting the dinner dishes done.

Most of them went into the dishwasher, a few had to be washed by hand. After hunting unsuccessfully for a pair of rubber gloves, she dipped her bare hands into the hot dishwater, something she hadn't done in years.

Jack prattled on as she did the dishes, and prattled on as she tidied the kitchen. It was just a superficial tidying; the room needed gutting from top to bottom and she certainly wasn't about to do it!

She had just finished when the phone rang.

Jack pounced on it.

And when he hung up, he said to Lacey, "The cria's here! Come on, Aunt Lacey, you've gotta see this!"

"No, I don't think—"

"Come on!" He grabbed her hand.

Lacey felt torn. Barns weren't her scene. But she did want to see Abigail. After all, the woman might be bringing up Alice's children. Wouldn't Alice want her to give the lady a once-over? Vet the vet, as it were?

Certainly she would!

She allowed Jack to pull her outside.

When they reached the barn door, Jack ran on ahead. She stepped forward, slowly.

The barn was dim and dusty and the floor was covered in hay, with more straggling from a roughly hewn manger. Apart from Sunflower and her new cria—wobbly, and with crimpy fleece the same tawny color as her mother's—there were no other animals around. Dermid was standing with his hands on his hips, relaxed, his eyes on the newborn, while the vet watched with a smile as the cria tried to find its feet.

"C'mon, Aunt Lacey!"

Dermid and the vet glanced around. Lacey saw surprise in Dermid's eyes.

"Hey," he called. "Come and meet the newest member of the family."

Lacey moved forward to join the group. She noticed that the vet's eyes held an expression of curiosity. She also noticed that the vet was very pretty indeed.

"Lacey," Dermid said, "this is our vet, Abby O'Donnell. Abby, my sister-in-law, Lacey Maxwell."

The redhead greeted her with a friendly "Hi, Lacey."

"Hi, nice to meet you, Abby." Lacey felt Dermid's eyes on her, and wondered if he was comparing her with Abby—and thinking, of course, how out of place she was here, with her cashmere sweater and expensive wool slacks and elegant Italian leather boots. "I'm glad the baby arrived safely."

"It was touch-and-go," Dermid said.

"What went wrong?" Lacey asked.

"Sunflower's so small," he said, "that the baby got stuck. I thought Abby might have to perform a Caesarean, but she managed to get her hands in to get a rope around the cria, and eventually pull her out."

Lacey saw that the mother was fussing over the cria, humming encouragement as the newborn tried to take a step.

"What are we going to call her, Dad?" Jack asked.

"Why don't we ask your aunt?"

"What do you think, Aunt Lacey?"

They all looked at Lacey as she sought for inspiration. Finally she suggested, "How about Topaz? She's the right color, and she's a November baby so it would fit there, too, since topaz is a November birthstone."

"I like it!" Jack nodded vigorously. "Dad? Abby?"

"Terrific," said Dermid.

"Cool!" said Abby.

So Topaz it was.

And soon afterward, Abby left.

Dermid still had chores to do so Jack and Lacey went back to the house and Lacey didn't see Dermid again until long after Jack had gone to bed. She was in the kitchen, heating a mug of milk in the microwave, when Dermid came in from outside. He brought in the frosty night air with him.

"Oh, you're still up," he said. "I thought you'd have gone off to bed by now."

"I'm going shortly," she said, "but I stayed up because there's something I want to ask you."

"What about?"

"About your vet."

"Yeah, what about her?"

"Jack's under the impression that you're going to marry Abby. If you are, I think I should know about it, because after all, whoever you marry is not only going to be Jack's stepmother, but she'll be bringing up the baby."

CHAPTER EIGHT

"JACK'S wrong," Dermid said. "I've no intention of marrying Abby O'Donnell."

"Well, not necessarily marry her...but...nowadays lots of couples just live together without—"

"Lacey, the woman's in a committed relationship with Mark Manley, one of the local sheep ranchers. What the devil made Jack think—"

"He overheard you saying to Arthur that Abby would make a top-notch rancher's wife. I guess," Lacey said, "he assumed you were talking about yourself."

"Well, I wasn't." He crossed to the sink, ran the hot water. As he washed his hands, he said, "I've no intention of getting married again."

"So you're really going to be bringing up your baby alone?"

"We've talked about this before, you *know* what my plans are." He rinsed his hands, and grabbing a towel from the rack, turned to face her as he dried them. "I coped with Jack after Alice died, I'll cope with his little sister. I won't be the first dad who's had to bring up a baby alone."

"Is that fair—especially to a little girl—to have to grow up without a mother?"

He tossed the towel down on the countertop. "Was it fair that *Alice* didn't live to see her children grow up?"

"No, of course not, but—"

"Look, Lacey, making the decision to have this baby be born at all was the hardest thing I've ever had to do." He crossed to the fridge. "And sure, there are going to be problems down the road but I'm determined not to anticipate them. I plan to take one day at a time, and I'd appreciate if you wouldn't come up with doom and gloom scenarios—"

"I'm sorry. Okay," she said. "One day at a time it is."

"Good girl!" He opened the fridge door and looked in. "You've done a good job here."

If Alice had been here, no matter how tired she might have been, she'd have busied herself making a snack for her man. Well, Lacey reflected, Dermid McTaggart wasn't *her* man, and she had no intention of busying herself for him at this or any other time of night!

Stifling a yawn, she said, "I'm going to bed."

He glanced around, his expression abstracted. "Okay," he said. "See you in the morning." And without further ado, he resumed his inspection of the fridge contents.

Contrarily she was peeved that he hadn't even *expected* her to make a snack for him.

"Good night," she said, and sashayed from the room, feeling unaccountably irritated. With herself.

The last thing she wanted was to become a slave to her brother-in-law. So why did she find herself wishing that she was a Cordon Bleu chef and could in the blink of an eye rustle him up a nutritious and delicious gourmet meal?

Next morning, Arthur arrived back at the ranch.

He loped into the kitchen just as Lacey and Jack were having breakfast. And when he saw Lacey, he stopped short. Then whipping off his battered, wide-brimmed hat, he stood there, a shy smile on his bony weather-beaten face.

"Hi, Ms. Maxwell. Sorry to barge in on you like this. I thought the boss might be here."

"He's feeding the animals," Jack said. "Arthur, Sunflower had her cria last night and Aunt Lacey named her Topaz." Scooping the last spoonful of cereal into his mouth, he scrambled from the table. "Let's go. You gotta see her..."

Arthur's solemn gaze moved to Lacey. "Will you excuse us, Ms. Maxwell?"

"Call me Lacey, Arthur." She got up from the table, too. "We're going to be getting to know each other pretty well over the next several months, we may as well get on a first-name basis right away, don't you think?"

"Whatever you say, Ms.—"

"Lacey."

He twirled his hat. "Right. Lacey."

"C'mon, Arthur." Jack was already at the door.

After they'd left, Lacey stuck the dishes in the dishwasher and gave the kitchen a cursory tidy. And then wondering how on earth she was going to fill the day, she wandered through to the sitting room.

Dead ashes lay in the grate. Dust covered every surface. Dirty mugs and a beer glass sat on the hearth. Old copies of the *Vancouver Sun* were piled on an ottoman.

And Scamp snoozed on the lint-covered carpet, in a patch of pale winter sunlight that had managed to penetrate window panes that were streaked with dirt.

Frowning, she roamed through the rest of the house, seeing the same signs of neglect everywhere—except for part of the bathroom she shared with Jack.

Earlier in the day, she'd scrubbed out the shower stall, and one of the sinks, and claimed that end of the vanity top for her own use. Jack was welcome to wallow in his stye, to leave black rings in the bath and wet towels on the floor, as long as he kept out of her space.

"It's your father's job to clean up after you," she'd told her nephew, who was watching her tidy. "Not mine."

"Wow!" he said, gaping as she set out her makeup. "What are all these bottles and jars and stuff for?"

"To make me beautiful."

"It must've cost you a whole bunch of money." Narrowing his gaze, he scrutinized her face in the mirror. "You must be real thankful," he said, "that it worked."

As a compliment it wasn't the most subtle she'd ever

had, but it was certainly the most original, and it had made her laugh.

It made her smile now as she remembered it, and she was still smiling when she returned to the sitting room.

There, she found Scamp had wakened and was stretching. Uncoiling himself, he got to his feet, and padding over to her, reached his nose up and licked her hand. Brown eyes fixed on her, he gave a sharp *"Wowf!"*

"What do you want?" she asked. "Walkies?"

He wagged his tail and gave a series of excited barks.

She bent down and patted him. "Right," she murmured. "Let's go for a walk."

Dermid saw her coming before she spotted him.

He'd left her in the kitchen with Jack a while back, and after feeding the animals, he'd noticed one of the fenceposts under the old oak tree had come loose, so he'd decided to shore it up.

He'd just finished the task when Lacey appeared.

The sun broke through a patch of white cloud, highlighting her as she approached. Black hair shining, lovely face peaceful, she crossed the grass with the easy glide of a cat. She was wearing a teal-blue jacket over a pale blue blouse and checked slacks, and she looked smart enough to be on the cover of a fashion magazine.

Too smart by far for this neck of the woods.

He wiped the back of his forearm over his brow, felt it wet with sweat. The morning was mild, but it wasn't the unseasonable warmth that was getting to him, it was this woman. This woman who was too smart, by far, for him.

But she stirred emotions he didn't want to feel. Last night, for example, when he was searching the fridge for something to eat, he'd been intensely aware of her. He'd been sorely tempted to turn around and haul her into his arms and kiss her...kiss away that cool elegance, find out what—if anything—lay below the perfect surface.

Instead he'd thrown her a deliberately vague glance. And she'd wasted no time in getting off to bed, obviously glad to be gone once she'd found out what she'd wanted to know: namely, that he wasn't going to marry Abby.

He moved out from under the shade of the oak tree, and he saw her eyes become wary when she noticed him.

"Hi," she said. "What are you doing?"

"Just fixing a fence post. Were you going anywhere in particular?"

"Scamp coaxed me into taking him out for a walk, but when he saw Jack and Arthur he decided to stay with them."

"Arthur's back?"

"Yes."

"Good. I phoned him last night," he added. "After

you went to bed. He said he had put his grandfather's place up for sale, and he'd be here sometime today."

"Will he be moving back into the house?"

"He says he'd prefer to have the log cabin."

"Where is it?"

"Down by the creek." Dermid waved a hand in the general direction. "Beyond that stand of trees. I was just going to check it out, haven't been there in a while. Want to come along?"

"Sure."

Together, they walked across the pastures, Dermid opening gates as they went, closing them behind them, to keep the grazing llamas and alpacas in their own fields.

"So," he said, "how are you feeling?"

"I feel absolutely fine."

You look fine. In fact you look terrific. And whatever that perfume is that you're wearing, it's really getting under my skin.

"Alice kept well, too," he said, "when she was expecting Jack."

"Yes, I remember."

"In fact, I don't think I ever saw her so busy. She was forever on the go—always cleaning and scrubbing and shining things up...and the garden, heck it was a showpiece. The way you get your face splashed around these fashion magazines, I used to tell Alice she could have got her house and garden splashed in some glossy magazine, too, if she'd wanted to. But it wasn't her style."

He'd brought Alice's name into the conversation in an effort to fill his thoughts with her, instead of with the woman swinging along at his side. But it wasn't working. It was impossible not to be aware of her, of her tantalizing fragrance, of the brush of her boots on the grass, the rustle of her jacket against her slacks, the silky swish of her hair as she flicked a hand through it.

"Oh, is that the place?" she asked. "It's pretty!"

It was just a simple cabin, with a neglected vegetable garden, and an ancient rosebush rambling up a cedar trellis by the door but though a city girl like Lacey might admire it, he mused, she'd never want to live in it. It was too Spartan by far for someone used to her glitzy life.

They walked up the dirt path to the door and he pushed it open and then stood aside for her to enter first.

"It's not fancy," he said. "But it's self-contained—electricity, running water, septic tank."

"And Arthur won't mind moving back in here?"

"He says he'd prefer it. He only moved up to the ranch house after Alice died to keep Jack and me company."

As she moved forward, he said, "I'll be right back. I just want to check that we haven't any uninvited guests."

"Mmm?"

"Rodents."

He went through to the kitchen, where he found no

signs of mice. Then he inspected the bathroom, the sitting room, and lastly went through to the bedroom.

She was there, standing at the window.

She didn't look round as he gave the room a quick check.

"Right," he said. "Everything seems okay, let's—"

"Dermid," she whispered, "come and see this!"

Eyebrows raised, he stepped across to join her, and on looking out, saw a deer in the vegetable garden. Poised light as a ballet dancer, ready to flee at the slightest sound, it daintily nibbled on something green.

An everyday sight for him; obviously not so for her.

They watched, together, until the deer suddenly leaped away, and took off through the nearby stand of trees.

Lacey's eyes shone as she looked up at him. "Wasn't that something?"

He only barely managed to stifle a groan. *She* was the one who was "something," It seemed to him that she was more beautiful every time he looked at her.

While watching the deer, he had braced himself by placing his hand on the wall to the side of the window. Now she was trapped in place by his arm.

And he wanted to keep her there.

"You're tall," he said.

You're *tall?* Where had that brilliant line come from!

She tilted back her head. "You've just noticed?" Her tone was teasing, but he detected a thread of nervousness in it. ''Fascinating. What else have you just noticed? My hair is black? My eyes are—''

''Green.'' He was going to kiss her. He knew it, and he knew he shouldn't, and he knew he wasn't going to be able to stop himself. But not quite yet. He wanted to look at her some more. Wanted to prolong the moment. An aching excitement was building inside him, and he felt the same overwhelming urge he'd felt in the kitchen last night, an urge to take her in his arms and hold her close, so he could feel every seductive feminine curve. ''Your eyes are green, and your nose is straight, and your lips—''

Her lips had parted. Her eyelids had flickered and opened wide for an instant...startled—but as he put his arms around her and pulled her to him, he heard a sharp inhiss of breath...and then her eyes closed, the sable lashes shadowing her cheeks.

When he kissed her, it felt sweeter than heaven. She was soft and scented and—after a breathy hesitation—so responsive he felt his self-control begin to unravel.

The kiss seemed to go on for ever. And with each passing second, he became more fully aroused.

She didn't fight him as he walked her back across the room, and eased her gently down onto the bed.

Nor did she protest when he lowered himself alongside her, and gathered her against him, feeling each pliant giving curve against his own hard solid flesh.

They kissed again. And again. She had flung one arm over the pillow, above his head; the other was around his waist and he could feel the tips of her nails clutching his shirt as she emitted tiny sounds—helpless little sounds. Sounds of surrender.

They unraveled what was left of his self-control.

He straddled her, on his knees. She stared up at him, her eyes smoky, her hair a black spill on the pillow. He fumbled with the buttons of her shirt. Opened them. And spread the flimsy silk fabric aside.

She wasn't wearing a bra.

Her breasts were creamy, full, the rosy nipples tightened to buds. Heart pounding, he ran the pad of his thumb over one quivering crest—and saw her throat muscles clench. She murmured something incoherent, eyes closing, head twisted to the side. He traced a fingertip over the swell of the breast, cupped it, caressed it, then slid his fingertip up over her collarbone, following the fine and delicate tracery of slate-blue veins—

Look, darling! Look at these tiny blue veins—I've never seen any there before, but I've read that they can show up early in pregnancy. Isn't it exciting!

Alice's words, Alice's voice, coming to him now, over the years. Jolting him into the past. He recalled the day, recalled the moment. He recalled the love and wonder that had been in her eyes. He remembered the shining love that had been in his own.

And here he was now, on the brink of tarnishing that memory.

With a low mutter of self-disgust, he grabbed the front of Lacey's shirt and pulled it together. And before she could possibly have had time to figure out what was happening, he lifted himself off her, twisted himself away and sat with his back to her, on the far edge of the bed. Sat with his head in his hands, as he struggled with his emotions.

The room was silent, except for his heavy breathing.

Then he heard the mattress sigh as she got up.

He heard her walk around the bed.

She stopped in front of him. He could see her long elegant feet, in their fine Italian boots; he could see the hem of her elegant designer pants.

And he knew she was looking down at him.

The least he could do was stand up and face her. Which he did.

He'd expected she might look flustered, or angry.

She looked neither.

But she did look pale, and she did look sad.

And that made it even more difficult for him to say the words that he knew he had to say.

"I'm sorry, Lacey." He lifted a hand in an appealing gesture. "I shouldn't have done that. It was—"

"It was a mistake. I understand." She met his gaze while she fastened the buttons he'd fumbled over just minutes before. "There'll never be anyone for you but Alice and you feel that by wanting to have sex with me, you're betraying her. Betraying the memory of what you had together. But the intimacy of the situation here, and my being...available...and maybe the loneliness in your heart—well, I guess it all came together in the moment, and it shouldn't surprise you that something like this happened. Don't beat yourself up over it. You're only human, just like everyone else."

"Don't make excuses for me, Lacey. I *am* sorry. Truly sorry—"

"You can be sorry on your own account, if you like. You can feel guilty on your own account, because of Alice, but please, Dermid, don't feel sorry on *my* behalf." She ran her hands through her hair and flicked it over her shoulders. "I'm a grown woman. I can look after myself."

And with that, she turned and stalked out of the cabin.

Lacey walked till she reached the crest of the hill, where she stopped, and with her hands in her pockets, looked unhappily out over the rolling pastures, at the patchwork of fenced meadows that chequered Dermid's estate.

She *was* a grown woman and she *could* look after herself. But even so, she had never wanted anyone as much as she had wanted Dermid a few minutes ago. When he had pulled away from her, she could have wept with disappointment, because his tender passion had promised her an experience such as she'd never had before. And for her, it would truly have been "making love."

For him, it would have been merely "having sex."

She had left him back in the cabin where he would, she mused, be wallowing in misery and memory, and despising himself for having given in to his lustful urges.

He'd felt the need for sex, and she'd been handy.

But when it came to the crunch, he couldn't go through with it. If he ever did let another woman into his life—which was doubtful—it would be somebody like Alice.

She herself was as different from Alice as anyone could possibly be—and not only in looks. She detested housework, she knew nothing about gardening, and when it came to cooking, to coming up with the kind of delicious meals that Alice had routinely produced, forget it!

No, she wasn't like Alice.

She could, of course, have learned to do all the things that Alice had done so well. She wouldn't have *liked* doing them; but she could have taught herself to do them. Take cooking. Following a recipe wasn't exactly rocket science...and she'd always been a quick study. It's just that she'd never been remotely interested in—

"Lacey."

Turning, she saw that Dermid had walked up behind her.

"What were you looking at?" he asked.

"Looking at?"

"You've been standing here for several minutes—"

"I wasn't looking at anything. I was just...thinking."

"Well," he said pleasantly, "you'll have lots of time

to loaf around and do that. I accept that unlike Alice, you're no great shakes as a housekeeper and I won't expect you to do much more than wash a dish once in a while. The next few months should be relaxing for you, so that after the baby's born you'll be able to go back to your life as a model, refreshed and energized."

He was acting as though their intimate interlude had never taken place; and he was also putting their relationship back on its earlier businesslike level. Fine. That was his prerogative.

But she'd felt her blood boil as she listened to him once again—*and once too often!*—compare her to Alice and find her wanting. She was not, however, going to let him see how furious he had made her.

"Yes," she said in a tone as benign as his own. "I'm sure I'll go back to work feeling rested and relaxed."

But she had no intention of just loafing around. The man was totally unaware that his idly dismissive comment, following on a myriad other such comments in the past, had acted, finally, like a spark to a tinderbox.

No great shakes as a housekeeper.

Well, we'll see about that! she thought, her head pounding with resentment.

And taking his trivializing comment as a direct challenge, she smiled at him guilelessly, even as she swept up the gauntlet he'd so unwittingly flung down.

CHAPTER NINE

THROUGH the night, the weather changed.

A wintry wind swept west from the Rockies, whistling around the chimney pots and rattling the garbage cans.

Lacey woke at dawn, and lay listening to the gale, and to the sound of the furnace as it pumped hot air into her bedroom through the heating vent.

Soon she fell asleep again, and when she next woke, she was shocked to find it was almost ten o'clock. Getting up quickly, she went into the bathroom and had a shower.

During the past weeks, she'd noticed her waist gradually thickening and the waistbands of her slacks becoming less comfortable; but this morning, when she caught sight of her naked body in the mirror, she saw, with a small shock of excitement, that her stomach was taking on a definitely rounded shape.

So far she'd been able to wear her regular clothes, but now she figured it was time to start wearing her maternity clothes, the gorgeous outfits she'd bought in New York, and which she'd packed to come to the ranch.

She decided on a loose-fitting green heavy-knit crew-neck sweater, over a black cotton turtleneck, paired with black maternity pants. She had just dressed, and slipped her feet into thin black socks and black ankle boots, when she felt an odd...shifting...in the region of her midriff.

Taken by surprise, she stood still.

And...there it was again! A definite shifting.

She set her hand over her abdomen—apprehensively, wondering if she'd jump a mile if she actually felt the baby move under her fingertips.

Oh! There it was again. And this time, she felt it wriggle right under her palm. Making itself more comfortable? Or trying to say "Hi!"?

Lacey felt overcome by awe.

Sinking down on the edge of the bed, she clasped her hands over her gently rounded mound and stared at them. Up till now, she'd never thought of the baby as a little person. It had just been an embryo, growing silently inside her.

But now—

A knock at the door jolted her.

"Yes?" she called sharply.

"Are you up? Dressed?"

It was Dermid.

"Yes, I'm—"

The door opened, and he stood there in a denim shirt and jeans, a concerned expression on his face. "You're usually downstairs by now. Jack and I wondered what—"

"The baby." She got unsteadily to her feet. "Dermid, it moved. I felt it!"

A smile inched over his face. "You're kidding! May I...?" he asked, gesturing toward her stomach.

She could hardly deny him the experience. It was, after all, his child. "Of course."

He walked over to her, and after pausing for an awkward moment, set his hand on her stomach.

Frowning, he concentrated.

She tried to concentrate, too. But he was too close. His head was too close. If she moved two inches, she could touch her lips to his springy hair, if she moved four inches, she could brush her lips against his hard jaw. But without moving at all, she could feel his body heat, smell his earthy male scent. She felt an ache of longing.

"Nothing," he murmured. "Not a flicker."

He looked up suddenly, his expression disappointed, but the instant their eyes met, his became guarded.

Lacey felt a dart of panic. What had he seen in hers? Too much, obviously, of what she'd been thinking.

She stepped away from him. "That's too bad," she murmured. "But...maybe next time."

He took a step toward her. "Lacey—"

Jack barreled into the room, his hair askew, his blue sweatshirt back to front, his jeans bagged down at the knees. "Dad, I'm ready for breakfast. You said you were going to make bacon and eggs. C'mon, I'm starving!"

And that was that. She would never know what Dermid had been about to say. Or do. She was left feeling like a baby bird, its beak wide open as its mother dangled a worm over it...and then flew away without giving it a nibble.

Frustrating to say the least.

And then, over breakfast, he announced that he was leaving next day to go to Oregon to pick up three llamas.

"I thought Arthur was going," Jack said. "You said yesterday that Arthur would be going."

"I've decided to go myself."

To get away from her? Lacey wondered. Had he just made up his mind a few minutes ago, when he'd seen the longing in her eyes? Had she frightened him into flight?

"How long will you be gone?" she asked.

"Three days. I'll leave early tomorrow, be back latish on Friday."

Well, it was an ill wind, she mused. With him gone, she would have three whole days to start carrying out her plan; she'd be able to scrub and dust and polish and window-clean without having to listen to any critical comments such as "That's not the way Alice did it!"

His trip couldn't have come at a more opportune time.

"I'd like to take you with me," he was saying now, "but I'll be driving over some rough country roads, and you'll be better off staying at home."

Oh, you fibber, she thought. The last thing you want is to be stuck in a van with me for hours on end.

"Can I come?" Jack asked.

"Sure." Dermid turned to Lacey. "That'll leave you totally free to do as you please during the day. And I'll get Arthur to sleep here at night, so you won't be alone."

"That won't be necessary. In fact," she said, as she saw Dermid was about to argue, "I'd much prefer to be on my own. It'll be more restful."

The word "restful" seemed to do the trick.

"Yeah," he said. "Okay, if you feel that way."

"I do. I'm used to being alone. I don't need anyone to look after me, I can look after myself!"

"Independent, aren't you!"

"Not stubbornly so. I don't mind asking for help when I need it, but in this case, I don't."

"No, I guess I'm the one who doesn't like to ask for help."

"You're right, there. I guess if it had been humanly possible, instead of having me act as a surrogate mother, you'd have wanted to give birth to this baby yourself!"

Jack looked interested. "What baby, Aunt Lacey?"

Lacey shot Dermid an apologetic look. He'd told her he'd tell Jack about the baby when he felt the time was right, and now she had put her foot in it.

He didn't seem fazed. "It's okay," he said to her. And to Jack, he said, "Your aunt Lacey's going to have a baby."

The child appeared to take the news in his stride. "Who's going to be the dad?"

"I am," Dermid said. But he added obviously

choosing his words with care, ‘‘Usually, when a baby comes, there’s a mom and a dad, and most times they’re married, and bring up the baby together, but in this case, it’s a bit different.’’

He hesitated, obvious at a loss as to what to say next, so Lacey decided to help him out.

‘‘What happened this time,’’ she said to Jack, ‘‘is that your mom and dad planned to have another baby, a little sister for you, but although the plan got started it didn’t get finished because your mom died.’’ She reached over and cupped her hands around his. ‘‘And since your dad really wanted this baby to be born, and because he knew your mom would, too, I offered to finish the plan for him.’’

Jack’s eyes brightened. ‘‘And then you and my dad will get married and we’ll all be a family again.’’

‘‘No, Jack.’’ Dermid’s voice was gruff. ‘‘After the baby’s born, your aunt Lacey will be going back to work and the baby will stay on the ranch with us.’’

‘‘You mean…it won’t have a mom?’’

‘‘That’s right,’’ Dermid said. ‘‘It won’t.’’

Jack looked bewildered. ‘‘A baby needs a mom. Everybody knows that! Every kid should have a mom.’’

‘‘Sweetie,’’ Lacey said, ‘‘this isn’t my baby. It’s your mom’s baby. I know it’s difficult to understand it’s growing inside me, but I’m just carrying it for her—’’

‘‘Well, she wouldn’t want you to have it and then not look after it. She’d want you to stay at the ranch and take care of it. If she was here, she'd have that baby and then she'd love it to bits! You shouldn't even *get* to have a baby if you're not going to stay around and be its mom."

"It's the way things have to be," Dermid said quietly. "Your aunt Lacey's doing us a tremendous favor by carrying this baby, and I'm very thankful to her. I'd like you to try to be thankful to her, too. What she's doing is very special and she's doing as much for us as she can."

Lacey heard weariness in his tone as he added, "Your mom loved babies, but you know that your aunt Lacey doesn't. You and I...and Arthur...will bring up this baby together, and you just wait and see, Jack. Your little sister is going to be the most loved baby that ever was."

Next morning, when Lacey got up and went through to the bathroom, she found that Jack was already there.

He was standing at the mirror, in blue cotton Y-fronts and a pair of navy socks. He had soaked his hair and plastered it flat to his head in an obvious attempt to tidy it, and now he was scrubbing his mouth with a damp face cloth. Noticing what looked like chocolate milk on his cheeks, Lacey said,

"Let me do that for you."

But as she made to take the cloth, he pulled back.

"I'd rather do it myself, Aunt Lacey. You're not going to be around here for very long, and I don't want to get used to you doing 'mom' things for me when you're not planning to stay after the new baby gets born.''

His tone was matter-of-fact, and without the slightest hint of criticism, but his words twisted Lacey's heart.

When she took him out to the van an hour later, he did, however, return her hug as usual with one of his own. Although in Jack's book face-washing was not permissible, being something only ''moms'' got to do, aunt-hugging, apparently, was still cool, for which she was thankful.

''See you on Friday, Aunt Lacey,'' he said as she closed his door. And she blew him a kiss.

Dermid had been in the barn giving Arthur some last-minute instructions. At that moment, he appeared, with Scamp at his heels, and his breath was white in the frosty morning air as he strode over to the van.

He was wearing a brown leather jacket over a denim shirt and jeans, and as Lacey gazed at him, taking in his rugged features, whiskey-brown eyes and rich dark auburn hair, she felt the oddest floating sensation.

And when he came to a stop in front of her, she felt a jolt of physical attraction that dismayed her.

''You're sure you'll be okay on your own?'' he asked, the faintest of frowns forming a V between his eyebrows.

''Yes, I'll be absolutely fine.''

''Well, take it easy when we're away.''

Jack yelled, ''C'mon, Dad!''

Scamp danced around Dermid, barking impatiently.

Dermid said, ''I'll be off then.''

Lacey followed him to the driver's side, and stood back as he opened the door. Lifting Scamp, he set him on the floor and the dog scrambled over to sit at Jack's feet.

Dermid then turned to Lacey. "We'll see you on Friday, then."

"Yes. Have a safe trip."

"You take care."

"I will."

He hesitated, as if reluctant to leave. Again, Lacey felt that odd floating sensation, but now it was more of a falling, falling, falling...

An icy gust of wind swept the forecourt, making her shiver.

"You'd better go on inside," he said. "It's bitter out here."

She stepped back. "And you'd better go, you have a long journey ahead."

He nodded, and climbed into the vehicle.

A few seconds later, he drove the van away down the road, and Lacey, hugging her warm green sweater around herself, watched it till it disappeared from sight, and then she hurried back into the house.

"You're not overdoin' it, are you?" Arthur asked when he came into the kitchen that afternoon and found Lacey with a mop and bucket of soapy water, attacking the kitchen floor. "Boss'll have my head on a plate if I let you tire yourself out."

Lacey stopped to take a breather. She'd gone to the

mall after Dermid left, and had bought cleaning supplies— along with rubber gloves to protect her hands—and when she came back she'd decided that the best place to start would be the kitchen. She'd been at it for hours! "Don't worry, Arthur. I miss going to the gym—this is good exercise."

He looked around. "You're making a great job. Haven't seen the place so spick-and-span since your sister..." His voice tailed away. Then before Lacey could say anything, he found his voice again. "The boss let it slide. He didn't have the heart for it. Well, grievin's a tough process, he didn't seem to care anymore."

"Well, I care, Arthur. I can't bear to see the house such a mess." And Alice would have hated it, too, but Lacey didn't say that. Besides, Arthur probably knew it already.

"Anything I can do to help, just let me know."

Lacey indicated two bulging green garbage bags by the kitchen door. "You could get rid of those for me," she said. "They're a bit heavy for me to be carting around."

"Sure." Arthur heaved up the bags, and as he left, said, "Just holler if you need me for anything else."

"I don't suppose you'd have time to wash the outside windows, have you?"

"Time?" He snorted. "I've been itchin' to wash them windows for months!"

"Oh, thank you, Arthur. That's about the only thing I don't feel up to tackling myself."

"I'll get to them first thing tomorrow." And with that, he departed, leaving her to get on with what she was doing.

Dinnertime had rolled around before she'd finished cleaning the floor to her satisfaction. After putting away the bucket and mop, she had a shower, and then made herself a chicken salad.

She ate in the kitchen, and though she felt exhausted, she also felt a tremendous sense of satisfaction as her gaze roamed around the squeaky-clean room.

Tomorrow morning, she decided as she forked a piece of tomato into her mouth, she would tackle the two bathrooms and the rest of the upstairs. And in the afternoon, she'd get to grips with the staircase and the slate-floored entry hall and the closet jammed with so much stuff the doors wouldn't close. And finally, on the third and last day, she would do a blitz on every other remaining nook and cranny in the house.

Yawning, she leaned back in her chair and feasted her eyes on the now cobweb-free ceiling.

It would be a pleasure, she mused, to see the expression on Dermid's face when he arrived home to discover she was fit for more than just loafing around.

Friday couldn't come soon enough!

"We're home, Jack." Dermid glanced at his dozing son, before pulling the van to a halt in front of the house. He could see that the main barn lights were on, and as he added, "Time to wake up," Arthur emerged through the open doors.

Jack murmured, "What time is it, Dad?"

"Way past your bedtime, son."

The kitchen light was on, too, and through the closed blinds, he could see a shadow moving.

Lacey's shadow.

As he anticipated seeing her again, despite himself he felt a fierce rush of excitement.

During the past three days, although he'd gone on the trip to create some distance between them, she'd never been far from his thoughts. When she'd seen him off, she'd looked so beautiful he'd had to fight an almost overwhelming urge to take her in his arms and kiss her. He'd felt dizzy from wanting her—wanting to hold her, wanting to whisper passionate words of seduction.

But he must never whisper those words. Even if he didn't feel so guilty for lusting after her, even if by some miracle she wanted him, too—and she hadn't seemed repulsed by him, that day at the cabin!—he must never give in to the temptation to have sex with her. He knew, deep within himself, that it would never be enough...at least, not for him. Once he'd taken her to bed, he'd want more. He'd want her to stay on at the ranch, after the baby was born.

But she was a career woman. First and last.

And heck, the woman didn't even like babies!

No, he must try to put her out of his mind.

He and Lacey Maxwell had no future together.

"Dad," Jack said, "are you and Arthur going to put the new llamas into the barn?"

"That we are."

"Do I have to help? I'm hungry."

"No, you go on in, let your aunt know we're back."

Arthur opened Jack's door and Scamp bounded down and took off into the bushes.

"Hi, Arthur!" Jack said, before running to the house.

"Everything okay while I was away?" Dermid asked, as they rounded the van to let the animals out.

"Sure," Arthur said. "Everything was fine."

"You kept an eye on Lacey?"

"Best I could."

"What does *that* mean?"

"She's one determined woman."

"And what does *that* mean?"

"Sorry, boss, can't say. But you'll find out for yourself, once you go inside."

Lacey sat at the kitchen table, ears cocked for the sound of the back door opening while she watched Jack wolf down a chicken and tomato sandwich.

"I thought you'd have stopped for something to eat on the way," she said.

"Dad wouldn't stop," Jack answered, and took another bite of his sandwich.

"He was in a hurry to get home?"

"He said you'd be bored and he wanted to get back to keep you company." He took a swig from his milk glass, and then ate the last crumbs of his sandwich.

Bored? She hadn't had *time* to be bored.

The click of the back door handle opening startled her and her nerves tightened. But when she turned around in her chair and saw Dermid come into the kitchen, in his leather jacket, and a navy plaid shirt and jeans, with his hair mussed and his jaw bristled, a wave of pleasure eased her tension.

"Hi." He took off his jacket, tossed it over a chair. "How have you been?"

"I've been fine," she said. "But how about you? You've had a tiring drive, you must be exhausted."

"A bit weary, but it's good to get back." He saw the plate of sandwiches on the table. "Are these for us? Terrific. Do you mind if I go up and have a quick shower first, wash all the road dust off me?"

Lacey said, "Go ahead."

Yawning, Jack got up from the table. He headed for the passage door. "I'm going to bed."

"Good idea, son. Lacey, I'll be right back. How about a pot of coffee?"

He followed Jack out to the passage without waiting for an answer. And Lacey heard him whistling as he ran upstairs, the sound decidedly cheerful. She didn't feel cheerful. *She* felt as deflated as a stabbed balloon.

He hadn't even noticed.

After all the hard work she'd done in the kitchen, the sheer *drudgery* of it, Dermid hadn't even noticed.

Lips compressed, she got up and put on the coffee. And then she took the sugar bowl from the cupboard, and set it, along with cutlery, a plate, and a mug, on the table.

After pacing the kitchen restlessly for a few minutes, she decided to go to bed.

It wasn't so very late, but all her physical activity over the past three days had caught up with her. And in sleep, she would surely forget her disappointment.

She was on her way upstairs when Dermid appeared on the landing and came running down toward her.

"Hey," he said, "you're not off to bed, are you?"

"Yes, I'm tired." They paused on the stairs as they met halfway. He'd changed into a fresh shirt and taupe pants, and his auburn hair was still damp. "I was up really early this morning."

But he didn't ask why she'd been up so early or what she'd been doing all day. He just said, "Better get some rest then. I hope you have a good sleep."

She nodded. And with a tight smile, walked past him and on up the stairs, saying "Good night," as she went.

"Good night, Lacey. And by the way," he called after her, "it's nice to come home to a clean house."

And with that, he headed for the kitchen, leaving her gaping after him. Stunned.

Nice? That was *it? Nice?*

Frustration pounded her head, making it ache.

And when she tossed aside the duvet and clambered into the center of her double bed a few minutes later, in her blue flannel nightie with the pattern of snow bears dancing, she lay limply on her back and let the hot tears flow.

Then, and only then, did she finally admit to herself what she'd closed her eyes to all along: she hadn't cleaned the house in order to *show* Dermid; she'd cleaned the house in order to *please* him.

And why had she wanted to please him?

Before she could come up with the right answer, a *rat-tat!* sounded on the door, and she froze.

"Lacey? It's me. Dermid. May I come in?"

"No!" She propped herself up on an elbow, and stared starkly into the dark, in the direction of his voice. "I'm asleep! Go away!"

But the door opened, and he came in, flicking on the light. The brightness dazzled her, and she threw herself back on the pillows, an arm over her eyes.

She heard the creak of a floorboard as he crossed to the bed. And her breath caught as he sat down beside her.

He was so close she caught the fresh scent of his soap and the minty flavor of his toothpaste.

"I'm so sorry," he said.

The remorse in his tone brought another rush of tears.

"About...what?" she quavered, through them.

"Arthur just told me...about you cleaning the house—"

"You knew it was clean," she said over a hiccup.

"Yes," he said softly. "I knew it was clean. How could I not notice! But I thought, you see, that you must have hired a cleaning company to come in. It never occurred to me that you'd done it all yourself. My God, Lacey, you must have slaved day and night to achieve what you did, and you completely transformed the place! Then when I was so offhand about it, you must have thought—''

Lacey sniffed, and dragging her arm from across her eyes, said, ''What I thought, Dermid McTaggart, was that you were the most unappreciative man on the face of the earth.''

''And now?'' he asked quietly. ''*Now* what do you think?''

But her emotional upheaval must have disturbed the baby, because it chose that moment to make its presence known by suddenly performing what felt like a back-flip.

''The baby!'' Frustration forgotten, Lacey beamed. ''It's moving again!'' She swept back the duvet. ''Here, put your hand here!'' She reached for one of his big hands and pulling him toward her, set it over her stomach, atop the flannel fabric with its pattern of dancing bears. ''There!'' She looked at him eagerly. ''Can you feel it now?''

His hand was warm, the pressure of it very light.

Lacey held her breath, willing the baby to move again.

And when it did, she heard her breath seep out, at the same time as Dermid murmured ''Wow!''

''Isn't it amazing?'' she whispered. ''Alice's baby...''

''It's awesome.'' Emotion made his voice husky. ''To be able to connect this way...''

He was sitting twisted awkwardly around, and it seemed the most natural thing in the world when—

without taking his hand from Lacey's stomach—he kicked off his boots, swung his legs onto the bed and lay down alongside her.

They lay like that, not speaking, enfolded in an intimacy that had nothing to do with sex and everything to do with love.

Contentment crept over Lacey, and gradually she relaxed completely. She felt herself begin to drift off to sleep, but she didn't try to stop herself. Being here, with Dermid beside her and Alice's baby between them, was a feeling like no other she'd ever known.

The bedroom was gray and shadowy when Dermid woke, and the wind howled eerily outside.

He realized he'd fallen asleep on Lacey's bed; and that sometime during the night, Lacey had pulled the duvet over both of them. They were cocooned together under it, and her body was close to his. She had an arm around him in her sleep, and he could feel the swell of her breasts against his shoulder, smell the feminine musky scent of her, hear the steadiness of her breathing.

Last night, sex had been the furthest thing from his mind, but now, he felt a stirring of desire.

Desire that intensified as she murmured in her sleep, and cuddled closer.

Torture, sheer torture.

What could be easier than putting his arms around her now, while she was drowsy, and ripe for seduction?

He'd never wanted anything more in his life.

Gritting his teeth, he slowly, very slowly and with infinite care, started to ease himself from under her arm.

She murmured again, this time in protest.

He slid free, and before creeping away from the bed, he tucked the duvet close to her warm body, so she wouldn't feel the draught left by his absence.

CHAPTER TEN

ARTHUR was in the kitchen, alone, when Lacey went downstairs that morning.

"I slept in," she told him. "What a sloth!"

"You prob'ly needed a good rest after guttin' the house out."

"Mmm." She filled the kettle, popped a couple of slices of bread into the toaster oven. "You're right about that."

"Bit of a misunderstandin' last night, about your cleanin'. Did the two of you get it all sorted out?"

"Yes, we did. Thanks to you." Taking a mug down from the cupboard, she said, "Where's everybody?"

"Boss took Jack into town to get him some new boots. He's in some fine good humor this morning." Arthur chuckled. "Never knew a man to be so lit up just 'cos his house got cleaned. If I'd have known it'd give him such a kick, heck I'd have cleaned it for him myself long ago!"

Lacey's heart gave a happy little lilt. She was pretty sure Dermid's good mood had nothing to do with the state of the house and everything to do with the little interlude in her bedroom. She'd been afraid that when he woke up and found he'd spent the night on her bed, he'd have been annoyed with himself. Apparently not.

She felt a warm glow inside her as she remembered how it had felt, in the predawn hours, to waken and discover him still there by her side. Like herself, he'd been exhausted and had drifted off to sleep. After flicking off the light, she'd lain in the dark, listening to him breathe, intensely aware of him, and deeply conscious of the peace it gave her to have him lying there with her.

Eventually she'd fallen asleep again. And when she'd wakened a second time, he was gone.

"Well, I'll be off now," Arthur said. "I just came in to put coffee on for the boss, he should be back soon."

The ranch hand left, and about half an hour later, Lacey heard the sound of Dermid's car.

She drank the last drops of her tea, and getting up from the table, put her breakfast dishes in the dishwasher and looked out the window.

It had snowed during the night; the faintest skifter of white laced the ground, and the car tires left a dark imprint as the vehicle approached the house.

Dermid killed the engine, and when he and Jack emerged, Lacey saw they were both wearing heavy parkas and jeans—and Jack was sporting a brand-new pair of boots.

The boy tore off to join Arthur who was in a nearby pasture training haltered llamas that would be used for carrying packs for hiking groups.

Dermid came straight into the house.

He smiled when he saw her. "Hi," he said. "You

finally got up! Did you have a good sleep...even with an intruder in your bed?''

She smiled back at him, and wanted to keep smiling. She could hardly believe how comfortable it was to be in this new stage of their relationship. Friendship...yet something more. More intimate. And how could it not be, after they'd spent the night together!

''I had a lovely sleep,'' she said, and added teasingly, ''At least you don't snore!''

He laughed. ''No, that's not one of my many faults. So...how's the baby today? On the move yet?'' Without waiting for her to reply, he crossed to her and setting one hand casually on her shoulder, set the other on her stomach and looked down at it. ''Hey, there—'' he tilted his head and cocked his ear as if expecting an answer ''—how's it going today?''

To Lacey's delight, the baby moved as if on cue. And Dermid was just as openly thrilled as he'd been the first time he felt it.

''That's my girl,'' he said, with affection softening his voice. ''You hang in there, we'll be seeing you before very long.''

Giving Lacey's tummy a gentle pat, he smiled at her again, and then moved over to the coffeepot, and poured himself a mug of coffee. He looked, she thought, like a man well satisfied with life.

Leaning back against the counter, he glanced around the kitchen. ''You know something?'' he said. ''This place feels like home again.''

It was the nicest compliment he could possibly have given her.

It more than made up for the three days of sheer drudgery, the protesting muscles, the aching arms, the broken fingernail. And it warmed her not only for the rest of the day, but for the days that followed, days that were among the happiest Lacey had ever experienced.

She knew, of course, that they couldn't last. This was Dermid's home, it could never be hers. This was Dermid's life, it could never be hers.

Her condo was always immaculate, kept that way by a cleaning company with whom she had a contract and she rarely lifted a finger herself. Yet she found herself enjoying the challenge of keeping the ranch house spick-and-span since she'd made it that way herself. And she found that teaching herself to cook could be a lot of fun, especially when the males she was cooking for were more than happy to sample all her efforts.

''Start with the simple stuff,'' Dermid had advised when she'd told him she was going to take over the kitchen.

''Like what?'' she'd asked, as she sat at the harvest table with a cookbook spread out before her.

''Well,'' he said, with an innocent look in his eyes, ''for dinner tonight, how about a nice minestrone followed by Salmon Wellington, and then for dessert, Black Forest Cake?''

''You'll be lucky,'' she retorted, ''if you get a boiled egg!''

But she found a lovely spaghetti recipe and although

it was fiddly, she made it, and served it with a green salad, and it was a great success.

Not so successful was the batch of fudge brownies she baked, since they sank in the middle, in a glistening brown sludge. But the edges were nice and crisp and salvageable, so she served slices of them with French vanilla ice cream and got away with it!

And she couldn't believe how relaxed she was. The years of modeling and traveling had been demanding, but only now, as her pregnancy progressed and she became as placid as one of Dermid's female llamas, did she fully realize just how much stress her career had put her under.

Still, at the back of her mind, she savored the prospect of returning to that life, and when she went into Nanaimo for her appointments with her gynecologist, she always stopped off to buy the current editions of *Glamour, Vogue, Elle* and any other fashion magazine she could find.

When Dermid saw her devouring them in the evening, as she sat with her feet up in the living room, he never said a word. He knew, as well as she did, that the moment this baby was born, the cord would be metaphorically, as well as literally, cut.

And he obviously had no problem with that.

In the meantime, the days rolled by pleasantly and soon it was mid-December and they were looking forward to the holiday season.

Felicity had invited them to Deerhaven for a family Christmas, along with all her other relatives on the island, but their plans went awry when a nasty 'flu bug felled Dermid and Jack at the last minute and Lacey had to phone and cancel.

"They're both in bed," Lacey said, as she sank onto a chair, with the kitchen phone at her ear. "Out for the count. I think they've got some sort of sleeping sickness! I can't even do a Florence Nightingale act because they don't want anything except lots of water!"

"Oh, it's so disappointing," Felicity said. "And what are *you* going to do? We can't have you sitting around on your own on Christmas Day! Why don't you come over by yourself—Arthur will do a good job of looking after them, he's done it before!"

"No, I'll stay," Lacey said. "I'd better stay."

Her brother was on the other line. "But Lace, you love parties, you're always the life and soul. And this one's going to be a zinger! Besides, aren't you missing the city life?"

He was teasing, but before Lacy could open her mouth to say, "Are you kidding? I'm going stir-crazy out here in the boonies!" a memory surfaced in her mind, the memory of her first evening at the ranch, when she'd felt so restless.

She remembered describing the feeling to Dermid, explaining that she felt something was missing, only she didn't know what. She'd thought then that what she missed was the busyness of the city, and the bright lights, and the excitement. And maybe it was. But strangely, she realized she missed none of those things now.

"Lace, are you still there?" her brother asked.

"You know," she said slowly, "the funny thing is I'm *not* missing the city life. I did, I really did, at first, but it's ages since I even thought about it."

"But aren't you bored?"

Lacey gave an amused laugh. "Bored? I don't have time to be bored. Believe me, looking after Dermid and Jack takes up every minute of my day, what with the cleaning, and the cooking—enormous meals, you wouldn't *believe* the appetites of those two!—and of course with them being outdoors with the animals most of the time, there's always a pile of dirty washing to do, and I do Arthur's, too, since he doesn't have a washing machine at the cabin, and then I've been painting the nursery pink, for the baby, and last week I found some bootee patterns and I'm learning to knit, and—"

Gales of laughter came from the other end of the line.

"What's so funny?" she asked. "What did I say?"

Felicity giggled. "Sure. And this is the woman who does a disappearing act when she hears the word: 'Cleanup?'"

And Jordan said, laughing, "Does Otto know that his top model's in danger of getting dishpan hands?"

They thought she was joking...and why wouldn't they! They'd never seen her do any of the things she'd mentioned, they'd only ever seen her "swanning around," as Dermid had often described it, in elegant clothes, looking beautiful, being charming—the vivacious visiting aunt, bringing presents from abroad. But giving nothing of herself.

And she was swamped by guilt as she recalled the countless times she'd visited Deerhaven and on arrival had offered to help...while already heading out to the patio to gaze idly at the view, or to the fridge to help herself to a glass of white wine, or to the pool to dive in for a lazy swim. Yes, she'd invariably offered to help...but without meaning a single word of it, knowing she'd never be taken up on her offer, because everyone knew that Lacey—with her immaculate hair and flawless makeup and red fingernails and designer clothes—didn't like doing household chores.

Oh, Fliss, she thought, how could I have taken advantage of you so! And how did you manage to entertain me with such seeming effortlessness, while you had that brood of children to look after and that huge house to run?

After she hung up the phone a minute later, she vowed that she'd never again take such hospitality for granted.

Christmas came and went—"a nonevent," as Dermid wryly described it once he was back on his feet.

But they did exchange presents—warm sweaters all around and a streamlined red sled for Jack.

And on New Year's Day, Lacey planned to cook a special turkey dinner and they invited Arthur to join them.

It snowed on New Year's Eve, the first heavy fall of

the winter, and the following afternoon, Dermid and Arthur took Jack sledding on Holly Hill, over by Arthur's cabin, and stayed out till darkness fell.

Then they had a hot chocolate at the cabin, and since Jack wanted to stay and help Arthur dry and store the sled, Dermid walked home, alone, in the dark.

As he approached the house and saw the kitchen light glowing, he could almost feel its warmth reach out through the cold to greet him.

Lacey's warmth.

It amazed him now that he'd ever thought her cold. And not only cold, but superficial. Useless. A pretty ornament. A bauble.

She was so very much more. And he dreaded the day when she'd be gone, back to her modeling career.

He'd never ever be able to repay her for what she was doing, having this baby for him. And she knew that. But what she didn't know, would never know, was that she had made him feel happy, and he'd truly believed, after Alice died, that he would never be happy again.

Lacey had lit up his life, and as she'd unknowingly dazzled him with her brightness, she'd let him see that there was an end to the grief he'd been struggling through.

He would always love Alice and cherish her memory, but he knew now that he was capable of loving again and for that, he would always be grateful to Lacey. Lacey, who was a city girl. Lacey, who wasn't interested in babies.

It was just his luck, he mused ironically, as he stamped snow from his boots and opened the back door, that since Alice's death, the first woman to catch his attention was the one woman in the world least likely to want it!

She was standing at the island, a cookbook open in front of her, her cheeks flushed with the heat coming from the oven.

She looked fabulous in a crimson smock top and narrow-fitting silver-gray slacks, with her ink-black hair scooped up in a loose topknot and feathery strands coiling free.

But she seemed flustered.

"Where's Jack?" she asked, her tone abstracted.

"At Arthur's. They'll be along shortly."

"Did you have fun sledding?"

"It was a blast." He hung his jacket on a hook by the back door. "Boy, does that turkey ever smell good!"

"I hope it's going to taste as good as it smells," she said, with an anxious *tsk.* "It's the first turkey I've ever cooked, and it won't be ready for a while as I was awfully late putting it in—"

"I'm sure it'll be fine—"

"I made stuffing," she said, "but I forgot to add the seasoning and—"

"Lacey, Arthur and Jack and I aren't expecting any gourmet meal—"

"I know you're not, but I planned it all so carefully and I wanted it to be perfect and now—"

To his dismay, tears welled up in her eyes. ''And I didn't remember—'' her voice cracked ''—I didn't even remember to buy cranberry sauce...''

He wasn't aware that he'd moved and yet before he knew it he had his arms around her, and was holding her close.

''Oh, Lacey,'' he murmured, his lips brushing her hair, ''please don't cry—''

''I'm hopeless,'' she sobbed. ''Such a failure. I've tried so hard to be a help here, but no matter how I try, I can never be Alice—''

''For heaven's sake!'' He grasped her shoulders roughly, and held her away from him. She looked up at him through tears of misery. ''Why on earth would you want to be Alice? What's wrong with being Lacey?''

''Oh, everything's wrong with being Lacey!'' Her words came out chokingly. ''I'm just hopeless—''

''Lacey.'' He slipped his arms around her and held her firmly. ''You're not hopeless. You're *amazing.* Believe me,'' he murmured, ''you're the most amazing person I know. I wouldn't change one single thing about you.''

And then, because disbelief shadowed her tearful green eyes—or maybe because he couldn't stop himself!—he kissed her.

Her lips were soft, and her breath tasted like honey. But she didn't respond—at least, for about five long seconds she didn't respond, and then, with a whispery sigh of surrender, she slid her arms around his waist and parted her lips for him.

The kiss was achingly sweet...

And it might have gone on for hours if the baby hadn't finally decided to object. What felt like a small kick—or a knee, or possibly an elbow—suddenly jutted into him, and the wonder of it diverted him as nothing else could have.

''Did you feel that?'' he murmured against Lacey's cheek.

She laughed shakily. ''A pushy little thing, isn't she! And determined to keep her father in line.''

He ran his hands up and down her back, caressing her, savouring the smoothness of her skin under the silk smock. ''Do *you* think,'' he asked, ''that I need to be kept in line?''

But as he waited for her answer, before she could speak the back door opened and Scamp shot in, barking madly, followed by Arthur and Jack.

The intimate moment was shattered—as so many of their intimate moments had been, Dermid reflected ruefully.

Jack insisted they all play a board game while they waited for the turkey to cook, and although they had a great time, with lots of laughter, and although Lacey was elated when the turkey dinner turned out to be just fine, he didn't have another chance to speak to her alone before she went to bed, leaving him sorely disappointed.

* * *

The following afternoon, when Dermid was busy with some accounting chores in his office, Felicity called.

"I need to speak to Lacey," she said. "I have a message for her, from her agent in New York. Otto. He's been trying to get in touch with her."

"She's gone up for a nap. I'll have her call you back."

"No, tell her to phone Otto. She'll be *so* excited," Felicity went on. "I expect you know that she had a fabulous offer from a company called GloryB, but she turned it down when you asked her to have the baby. Anyway, it seems they may still be interested in her, when she's ready to go back to work. Will you tell her?"

"Sure. Sure I will."

"We're looking forward to seeing you all next month. You're still planning on going to Skye at the end of February for your parents' fiftieth anniversary party? You and Jack?"

"Yeah, I'm still planning on it. My parents wanted me to bring Lacey, they're so thrilled about the baby, and I'd love to have taken her with me, but I decided it wouldn't be a good idea."

"I think you're wise, she'll be well into her pregnancy by that time. It's a long flight and who knows, there's always the chance she could go into labor en route—not a risk you'd want to take."

"Fliss, about that original offer from GloryB, the one Lacey turned down, she never made any mention of it to me. Obviously she didn't want me to know. Forget you ever told me, okay?''

''Of course.''

Later, after he hung up the phone, Dermid sat back in his chair and stared starkly into space. Lacey had made that huge sacrifice? And had kept if from him?

He already thought she was an amazing woman.

But what he had just learned really blew him away.

''I'll have to call him at home,'' Lacey said when Dermid told her Otto had phoned Deerhaven looking for her. ''With the time difference, I doubt he'll still be in his office. I wonder what he wants?''

They were standing at the foot of the stairs, where Dermid had caught her when she came down from her nap.

He said, ''Use the phone in my office.''

''Thanks.''

''Did you sleep?''

''I tried to but somebody—'' with a smile she ran a hand over her bulge ''—*this* little somebody, wanted to play!''

Lacey thought he might chuckle, but he was looking at her as if he wasn't listening to what she was saying. As if he had his mind on other things.

And then, totally out of the blue, he said, ''Lacey, I hope you know how grateful I am, for what you're doing.''

He sounded so humble she felt a lump in her throat.

''Oh, Dermid, you don't have to feel grateful. We're

in this together, and I know that when I look back on the whole experience, I'll feel nothing but joy…and my own gratitude, to you, for letting me do this for Alice."

Impulsively she reached up and kissed his cheek.

And then, her heart overflowing with emotion, she turned away from him and went into his office.

Closing the door, she slumped back against it.

She felt so much love for him, she could hardly bear it. But it was a hopeless love, and she would have to try her very best to accept that.

What a different man he was, though, from the man who for years had kept her at a distancc. She'd thought him hard, then, and arrogant. Now she knew he had a heart as soft as mush, and he was one of the most wonderful and caring people she'd ever met.

But he was not, unhappily, for her.

So she'd better get on with the life she had chosen.

She phoned Otto, and he answered on the fourth ring.

"It's GloryB," he told her, over a hubbub of voices. "They still want you, Lacey. Marlyse took over after Kinga retired, but she's already broken the terms of her contract and the GloryB lawyers are suing. It'll take a while for the dust to settle, but when it does they're going to be approaching you again. They're not going to put pressure on you, they're going to wait and offer you a contract once the baby's born. I just wanted you to know…"

Children's laughter came over the phone, and then voices singing, "Happy Birthday..."

Otto said, "Gotta go, I'll be in touch, sweetie."

Lacey sat back in her chair after she'd hung up the phone, and rested her hands on the mound of her stomach.

It was all going to happen, she thought dazedly. She was going to have the whole ball of wax after all. Fate had not only given her time off to have her sister's baby, she was going to achieve her career goal, too.

When she went through to the sitting room, she found Jack and Dermid watching TV.

Dermid looked up. And when he saw her beaming face, he said, "Good news?"

"Wonderful," she said. And went on to spill out what Otto had told her.

Dermid seemed very pleased for her. And she knew it was for the best, because although she loved him, and though she was enjoying being at the ranch now that she had the house running smoothly, being a stay-at-home mom caring for a new baby was not what she wanted.

So why, then, when she'd just had the most fantastic news in her life, did she suddenly feel so let down!

"So," Dermid said, "how's everything going?"

"Really well!" Lacey clutched his arm as he walked her from the medical clinic to where his car sat in the parking lot. It was the beginning of February, and although the snowfall had long since melted away, it had been frosty overnight and in places the ground was slippy. "Dr. Robinson says she's a big baby and that if we didn't know our dates for sure, he'd have sworn I was further on than I am!"

"When does he want to see you again?"

"In three weeks." She beamed up at him, her eyes sparkling. "The twenty-third."

He thought he'd never seen her more beautiful. Her coat was scarlet and the icy wind painted her cheeks red and blew her black hair into glossy black ribbons.

Her lips were breathlessly parted, and he yearned to kiss them. But he restrained himself. When she signed her new GloryB contract after the baby was born, it would draw her back to her old life. And if he had ever fooled himself into thinking he might compete with her career, her exhilaration after talking with her agent had dashed any such hopes to smithereens. And he had decided, there and then, to detach himself from her emotionally, as he was only going to lay up more heartache for himself if he built up more memories to torture himself with once she was gone.

So now he said, lightly, "The twenty-third. That's no good. I won't be back from Scotland till the twenty-fourth, and I want to be here to drive you. Phone the clinic when we get home, change your appointment to the twenty-fifth."

"Dermid, I'm perfectly capable of driving myself, I do wish you wouldn't fuss—"

"I'm not fussing." They'd reached his car, and he

unlocked her door. "It's just that the roads can be tricky at this time of year and—"

"I've been driving since I was sixteen!

"I won't enjoy myself for one single minute when I'm away if I have to worry about you."

"That's blackmail!"

"Yeah." He grinned. "I know. But is it going to work?"

CHAPTER ELEVEN

LACEY laughed. "Yes," she said. "It worked."

And when they got back to the ranch, before she even took off her coat, she phoned and changed the date of her appointment.

"There," she said to Dermid as she put down the phone. "*Now* will you enjoy the anniversary party?"

"As much as I can, under the circumstances."

"What do you mean?"

"I don't like to be away so close to the baby's birth."

"It's not close, the baby's not due till the end of March! Besides, you'll only be gone for a few days."

She'd said "only," but she was going to miss him terribly. Lovely though it would be to spend the time at Deerhaven, the down side was that Dermid wouldn't be there and she wanted to spend every moment with him.

Time was passing too quickly, frighteningly quickly. Before she knew it, her months at the ranch would be just a memory—a memory that would remain a bitter-sweet one for the rest of her life.

"That was a heavy sigh!" Dermid said. "Are you tired? You go up to bed, I'll bring you a cup of tea and then you can have your nap."

"Thanks," she said. "I'll be glad to get off my feet. But could you make it hot milk instead?"

On the way to her room, she detoured by the nursery. And pausing, she leaned against the doorjamb, looking at the pink walls, remembering how Felicity and Jordan had laughed when she said she'd painted them. Well, she *had* painted them herself, and scrutinizing them now, she decided she had made a darned good job of it.

But Dermid was the one who had taken Jack's crib down from the attic and scrubbed it, and he was the one who had put up the pink and white curtains Felicity had given them, and he was the one who had installed the new pink carpet.

And it was Jack who had so generously donated some of the nicest soft toys from his collection, and the nursery rhyme bedside light which he said he'd outgrown, and the wall-hanging Felicity had quilted when he was an infant.

And soon, Lacey thought, Alice's baby girl would lie in that crib, and enjoy this pretty room.

She cupped her hand over her bulge. Alice's baby. It was odd that she had never come to think of it as her own baby. Yet, not odd, considering that she'd never had any desire to have a baby of her own. What she felt for this one was kinship and caring…a family fondness, because any child of Alice's would automatically have had that—

"Penny for them."

Lacey turned her head and saw Dermid standing on

the landing, watching her, a steaming mug of milk in his hand.

"I was just thinking," she said, "how sad it is that when you bring your baby home from the hospital Alice won't be here to see it."

"I notice you don't say when *we* bring the baby home. You're still planning on handing the child over to me as soon as it's born, you won't even come back here for a few days, just while you get your strength back?"

Lacey shook her head. And pushing herself from the door jamb, said, "No, my job will be done. I'll have played my part. After that, it'll be totally up to you, Dermid. And I know you'll do a wonderful job of bringing this baby up. Just as you've been doing with Jack."

"And you'll be the face of GloryB. So we both get what we want."

They walked into her room, and he set the mug on the bedside table. She felt comfortable enough with him now that she slipped off her shoes and her slacks in front of him. Then she flipped back the duvet and clambered into bed. He plumped up her pillows and adjusted them, and as she sat back against them, he pulled the duvet over her, and tucked her in.

She felt cosy. And cosseted.

He handed her the heavy ceramic mug, and she wrapped her hands around it. "Thanks," she said. And looking up at him, she said, softly, "You're so good to me, Dermid."

He leaned over and kissed her brow, with a gentleness that made her heart hurt.

"How could I not be good to you, Lacey? You're giving me a gift that I'll cherish for the rest of my life."

She saw tears in his eyes, which made her heart hurt even more.

And when he walked out of the room, closing the door behind him, she felt her own tears start to flow, and she did nothing to stop them.

Dermid asked Arthur to move back to the ranch house while he was in Scotland.

"You don't have a phone at the cabin," he said. "And I'll be phoning you from time to time so there'll be more chance of catching you if you're living at the house."

So it was arranged that Arthur would move in the day they left.

The night before, Lacey went into Jack's room to pack his clothes.

She found him sitting cross-legged on the bed, in his pyjamas, sorting through a pile of books and toys, trying to decide which to take with him.

But when he chanced to glance up and saw her packing the new navy blazer his father had bought him for the trip, he said, with a scowl, "Do I *have* to take that?"

"Yes, you have to look nice at the party."

"Me and my dad aren't *party animals,*" he said,

obviously relishing the sound of the phrase as he rolled it around in his mouth.

Dermid appeared in the doorway. ''No, we're not, son, but as I've said to you before, when it comes to family, we have to make the effort.''

''How's *your* packing coming along?'' Lacey asked him.

''I've thrown some stuff in a weekend bag,'' he said. ''I'm all set to go.''

''Kilt and all?''

His grin widened. ''Kilt and all. Haven't worn it since my wedding day, but it'll give the old folks a kick.''

''What time are we leaving tomorrow, Dad?''

''Our flight leaves at four o'clock. We'll get the ferry over in the morning and be in time for an early lunch at Deerhaven. And then Jordan's going to drive us to the airport.''

''Will you come and see us off, Aunt Lacey?''

''Of course, if you want me to.''

''Yes, I do. But it's lucky you aren't coming with us on the plane, I don't think you'd fit into the seat.''

Lacey laughed. ''You're right about that,'' she said. ''This sister of yours isn't so little anymore.''

''Well, that's good,'' Jack said, ''because when she gets here I want to be able to play with her. I can't wait!'' He looked at his father. ''What's her name gonna be, Dad?''

''I haven't given it any thought,'' he said. ''How

about all three of us pick a name, give her three names?''

''Yeah,'' Jack said. ''Let's! Aunt Lacey, what name do you choose?''

Lacey hesitated, but Dermid said, ''Go on.''

''Then,'' Lacey said, ''I'd like to call her Alice.''

Dermid's eyes softened as he looked at her. ''Good girl,'' he said. ''And then my choice will be Lacey, since without Lacey, there would *be* no baby.''

Lacey felt as warmed as if he'd given her a huge hug. If ever she had doubted that Dermid's affection for her was genuine, his words had dispelled it. Her smile was misty, and with it she showed him her gratitude.

''Now my turn,'' Jack said. And jumping up and down on his bed, he said ''I want to call her Jill, and then we'll be Jack and Jill and that will be really truly cool!''

Dermid chuckled. ''It's cool all right. So,'' he said, ''it'll be Alice Lacey Gillian McTaggart.''

''But,'' said Jack, jumping extra high, ''we'll call her *Jill!*''

''Yes,'' his father said, and caught his son as the boy leaped toward him, like a sprawling frog, off the bed. ''We'll call her Jill.''

And so it was that Alice's daughter was named.

Next morning, Arthur saw them off, and they drove to the ferry in brilliant sunshine.

The ferry trip was uneventful, and when they arrived

at Deerhaven, Felicity and Jordan had prepared a delicious lunch for them.

Right after lunch, Jordan set out to drive them to the airport. Traffic was heavy en route, and by the time they reached the terminal, and Dermid and Jack had checked in, it was time to get along to the departure gate.

Before Dermid and Jack went through security, Jordan took out his wallet and said to Jack, "Here's a little something for you to spend while you're away..."

Meanwhile, Dermid turned his attention to Lacey.

"Well," he said. "This is it. I wish I didn't have to leave you alone."

"I won't be alone," she said.

"You know what I mean." His eyes were as dark today as his brown leather jacket. He was carrying his weekend bag; now he dropped it. And Lacey's heart gave a little jump when he stepped forward and grasped her shoulders.

Eyes locked with hers, he said huskily, "Take care."

She swallowed as emotion tightened her throat. "You, too."

He took in a deep breath, and then kissed her cheek, tenderly, before pulling back and releasing her. He smiled, but it was just a curving of his lips. She had never seen his eyes more serious.

"Lacey—"

"Dad!" Jack tugged his father's jacket sleeve. "Are we going now?"

Lacey saw a flicker of frustration in Dermid's eyes,

and wondered if was thinking—as she was—how often Jack had interrupted them at untimely moments. Then he gave her a wry smile, and ruffled Jack's hair affectionately.

"Yup," he said, "we're going now."

He and Jordan said their goodbyes, and then Jordan took Lacey's hand and they stood back while Dermid and Jack walked away from them, through the security gate.

If Dermid waved as they took off along the passageway leading to the departure lounge, Lacey wouldn't have known.

It was impossible for her to see, for the veil of tears that blurred her eyes.

Jordan was very quiet on the drive home, which suited Lacey because she wasn't in the mood for chatting.

But when he drew his car to a halt outside Deerhaven, he turned in his seat and looked at her.

"You're in love with him," he said.

"No," she said, almost gasping the denial. "I'm not. Of course I'm not."

"Yes," he said. "You are."

She brushed a hand over her eyes. "Jordan, don't—"

"What's happened between the two of you, Lace? You used to be forever sniping at each other. Now...today...I sensed something very different going on..."

"We've become friends, that's all." Lacey felt as if she was choking. "We're friends, very good friends."

"But you do love him."

Eyes swimming, she said, on a ragged breath, "It's hopeless, Jordan. It could never work. He'll never get over Alice...and as for me, you know how much I enjoy my career. And babies, I'm not interested in babies, when this one's born, I'll have no qualms about handing it over—"

"You're sure?"

"Absolutely."

He sighed. "Then I guess you're right, it is hopeless. But at least you've become friends, and that's something to be grateful for."

It *was* something to be grateful for; but Lacey knew, in her heart of hearts, that for her, at least, it would never be enough.

"These four days have just flown past," Felicity said as she sat on the edge of Lacey's bed on Thursday night, having just brought her a mug of cocoa and set it on the bedside table. "Tomorrow Dermid and Jack will be back, and this time tomorrow night, you'll be at the ranch again."

Lacey didn't think the four days had flown past; for her, they had dragged. She'd felt listless and out of sorts, and her back had ached constantly, but it wasn't only that. Although she'd enjoyed being with Felicity and the rest of the family, she'd missed Dermid terribly.

The separation had intensified her dread of the more permanent separation that lay ahead, after she'd delivered Alice's baby and handed it over.

Almost as if she'd read Lacey's thoughts, Felicity said, out of the blue, ''If the baby looks anything like Alice, she'll be a dear little thing.''

''Yes, she will.'' Lacey reached for her cocoa, and holding the mug in both hands, took a sip. ''But if she has Dermid's coloring, that would be glorious, too.''

They chatted for a bit, until Lacey had finished her drink. Felicity took the mug from her, and stood up. ''You get some sleep now. Are you going to the airport with Jordan tomorrow afternoon to pick them up?''

''I think I'll stay here and have a nap. Dermid'll want to get right back to the ranch, so I'd be better to have a rest after lunch. The ferry trip can be tiring.''

''Good night, then, Lacey.'' Felicity bent over and gave her a peck. ''See you tomorrow.''

Lacey cuddled back under the bedcovers. ''Yes, good night, Fliss. And thanks for everything.''

''Thank *you,* Lacey. I really appreciated your making dinner tonight—the meat loaf was fabulous, even picky little Todd ate every scrap on his plate. And to think that Jordan and I laughed at you back then when you said you'd been cooking and cleaning—we're both really impressed, Lacey, and very proud of you.''

''Don't be too impressed!'' Lacey said. ''I'm not like you, I can't say I've always *enjoyed* what I was doing!''

''Cleaning toilets? Scrubbing floors? Scouring pans?''

Felicity's eyes twinkled. "What's to enjoy about that!"

Lacey giggled.

And then Felicity left, with a soft, "Sleep tight!" as she flicked off the light.

Lacey did sleep tight...but only till three in the morning, at which time she awoke with a dagger-sharp pain in her back. A pain that took her breath away. A pain such as she'd never experienced before.

Surely she wasn't going into labor?

Shocked, aghast, she sat bolt upright in bed, and switched on the light. She couldn't be in labor. It was far too soon. The baby wasn't due for weeks yet—

But the pain wasn't going to go away. It came back fifteen minutes later, and then, not too long after, it came back again. And each time, she felt as if a red-hot hand was grabbing her insides, and twisting them till she wanted to scream.

Feeling wobbly, and terrified, and fighting a rising panic, she got up and put on her robe and made her way through to the master bedroom. She knocked on the door and when Jordan called "Come in," she opened the door.

"It's me," she whispered into the dark. "Something's wrong." Her voice was as wobbly as her legs. "I think I'm in labor."

Light flooded the room, and blinking, she saw Felicity leaning toward her bedside lamp, while Jordan lurched out of bed. He was at her side in a second, and Fliss was there two seconds later.

They led her back to her room, and Felicity sat her on the bed. "I'll get you dressed," she said, calmly and reassuringly. "But first, what was your doctor's name, the one at the clinic?"

Lacey told her.

"Jordan, get a hold of him on the phone, tell him what's happening, ask him which hospital Lacey should go to..."

Competently, after Jordan hurried off, Felicity dressed Lacey, packed a few things in a bag, and put an arm around her when another contraction grabbed Lacey around the middle.

"You're going to be fine," Felicity said. "Your contractions are nicely spaced out, you have loads of time. But you'd best get to the hospital as soon as possible, because you'll feel much more relaxed once you're there..."

Felicity kept up the reassuring chatter but for Lacey she might as well have been speaking double Dutch for she took little of it in.

All she could think of was the baby. It was too early. If it was born now, would it survive?

"Dad, you said Uncle Jordan would be meeting us when we came back. Where is he?"

Dermid heaved his weekend bag from the luggage carousel and sent a searching look around. No sign of his brother-in-law.

"Maybe he had a meeting and couldn't get away."

"Can you phone and find out?"

"Yeah, I'll call Deerhaven."

But when he did, an unfamiliar voice answered.

He said, "Who am I speaking to?"

"Is that Mr. McTaggart?"

"That's right—"

"It's Shauna, the baby-sitter. Mrs. Maxwell asked me to tell you, if you phoned, that she and Mr. Maxwell are over at Lions Gate Hospital. Lacey—Ms. Maxwell—went into labor last night and she's having her baby. At least, it hasn't arrived yet—"

Dermid felt as if his heart was going to explode. "Lions Gate?" he repeated, dazed. "In labor?"

"And she said could you take a cab as they don't want to leave—"

"Thanks. I'm on my way."

He slammed down the phone and grabbing Jack's hand started through the airport at a run.

"What is it, Dad?" asked a breathless Jack. "Is something wrong?"

"Your baby sister's on her way," Dermid replied, hardly able to hear himself over the pounding in his ears. And as he ran, he recalled how Lacey had fallen to pieces at Christmas because she'd forgotten to buy cranberry sauce. What to most women would have been a minor incident, for her had been a major disaster.

She'd tried her best, but it was obvious she couldn't cope in a crisis. And what could be more of a crisis than going into labor for the first time, without the baby's father to support her, and five weeks early to boot.

He would never forgive himself for not being there for her when she needed him most.

And she, no doubt, would never forgive him.

"Come on, Lacey, you can do it! One last push, just one last push..."

Soaked in sweat and wilted with exhaustion, Lacey drew on her last ounce of remaining strength to do as the doctor ordered. She drew in the deepest breath she had ever drawn, and pushed the hardest she had ever pushed. Pushed, pushed, pushed, the exertion straining every muscle, swelling every blood vessel to near-bursting point...

And then, like jelly squeezed from a tube, the baby slipped out. One moment, Lacey was giving everything she'd got, a gargantuan effort...and the next, the glorious wonderful next, it was over. It was all over.

The baby was born.

And as Lacey lay there, sweat-drenched and in shock, she heard a thin rising wail. The baby's first cry.

It clenched something deep in her core.

And brought tears to her eyes. She had shed more tears, she thought weakly, during the months of her pregnancy than during the whole of the rest of her life.

The following minutes passed in a hazy blur. She could hear the murmur of voices, was conscious that the baby had been whisked away, but she was too numb to think. All she could do was "be," while someone washed her and brushed her hair, and put her in a fresh nightie.

She must have dozed a little, for the next thing she knew, she was being wheeled along a long corridor, and into a small room, and lifted onto a hard bed.

Then Jordan and Felicity appeared hand in hand at her bedside.

She lay back, hardly able to keep her eyes open, and let their congratulations wash over her. She tried to smile, but she was too tired.

"I think we should let her sleep," she heard Felicity whisper. "And you should phone home, see if..."

She didn't hear anymore, as her eyelids closed and she drifted off into another world.

Next time she woke, it was to find a nurse standing by her bed.

"Ms. Maxwell, I'm sorry we took so long, but we had to check your baby out thoroughly. You'll be relieved to hear that she's fine, although she won't get home right away—we're going to keep her in the special care nursery for a few days till she gains a little more weight."

Lacey sent up a fervent prayer of thanks. "That's wonderful news," she said. "Thank you so much."

"I understand you're not planning to breast-feed the infant, so I'm going to bring you some cabbage-based gel, it'll help ease any discomfort and cool your skin. And you must be dying for a cup of tea." The nurse helped her to a sitting position and Lacey leaned back against the pillows. "In the meantime..."

Lacey hadn't noticed the small cot at the foot of the bed. And when the nurse lifted the baby, she felt a heartbreaking wave of sadness.

Alice's baby. But her sister hadn't lived to see her little girl being born.

Feeling teary, she reached up to take the baby.

"Thank you," she said. "Just leave her with me for a little while."

The nurse bustled away, leaving Lacey with the sleeping baby nestled in her arms. A scrap of a thing, enfolded in a pink blanket. And weighing next to nothing.

Lacey hadn't held an infant since Felicity's youngest was born and though she'd thought her nephew was cute enough despite his red scrunched-up face and bald pate, she had felt no great surge of love for him. That hadn't come till later, when he was finally old enough to communicate.

This baby was neither red nor wrinkled nor bald. Alice Lacey Gillian McTaggart had silky black hair, smooth skin, a perfect little nose and a mouth just made for blowing bubbles. Eagerly Lacey searched her small face for signs of Alice, but saw none. Searched for signs of Dermid, but saw none of him, either.

Dermid.

Her pulse picked up pace as she anticipated seeing him. He'd be over the moon when he found out that his daughter had arrived safely. And when he saw this sweet infant, he'd be crazy about her—

The baby stirred, and started to cry.

"Hush," Lacey whispered, and rocked her.

But the crying continued. Became louder. More demanding.

Lacey felt a sudden tingling in her nipples, and then as if on cue, the child started rooting for her breasts.

Dismayed, Lacey said, "No, sweetie, you can't!"

But the baby was not about to be denied. She wanted to suck, and suck she would.

"Sweetie, darling, no..."

But even as she said the words, Lacey felt a rush, an aching need, a primal urge to give succour to the now frantically seeking infant. Her breasts were swollen, the nipples throbbing, and with a feeling of distress, she noticed that the front of her nightie was damp.

The baby was sucking the moist fabric, intensely focused on her pursuit of sustenance.

Fighting panic, Lacey struggled with herself—she knew she mustn't feed this baby, for if she did, her soul-deep instinct told her it would tie her to the child forever. But how could she humanly deny her nourishment!

It was too much, the decision too hard—

But then the decision was taken out of her hands.

Or was it?

Afterward she would never be sure if the baby had somehow worried its way through a gap in her nightie, or if she, Lacey, had pulled the nightie aside, but before she knew what was happening, the baby had latched onto her nipple and was feeding as ravenously as if her very life depended on it.

Lacey cradled her tenderly, and felt a delicious relaxation creep over her. It felt good. It felt right. It felt natural. And if she was making a mistake, she'd have to suffer the consequences. Later. She couldn't think about that now. She closed her mind to it.

Then after several minutes of voracious gobbling, the infant slowed down, and sucked more gently, as if for comfort now rather than in a search for food.

"There," Lacey whispered, and kissed the baby's brow, inhaling the baby's lovely milky scent, "how was that?"

At the sound of her voice, the baby opened her eyes. Dark blue eyes, round, solemn, and filled with wisdom.

They met Lacey's unblinkingly, stared up at her, stared right into her, and as Lacey gazed back into the midnight-blue depths, she knew this child was acknowledging her as her mother. And she knew, for the first time and at last, that babies could communicate from the moment they were born, and in a way that had no need for words.

"Oh, my precious precious baby." Lacey kissed her daughter's cheek, tasted it sweet with her own milk. "I love you, my darling. And I'll never ever give you away."

When she raised her head, she saw that the child's

eyelids had closed and she had fallen asleep at her breast.

At the same time, she sensed someone watching her.

Her heart almost stopped when she saw Dermid in the doorway.

How much had he seen? she wondered.

And what was even more crucial, how much had he heard?

CHAPTER TWELVE

DERMID knew he would never forget this moment.

He hadn't expected to see Lacey with the baby. And he certainly hadn't expected to see her with the infant at her breast. The sight brought tears to his eyes. She had been so supremely confident she wouldn't get emotionally attached to the newborn...but now? What did it mean?

"You look fantastic," he said, almost afraid to breathe as he tiptoed across to the bed. "I met Jordan and Fliss downstairs, they told me that it was a very difficult birth and you were amazing. Lacey, I'm so proud of you, but so sorry I wasn't here to give you support—"

"Your daughter's impatient!" Pushing back a hank of limp hair, she smiled up at him. Aglow. "How were we to know she wasn't about to wait for her due date!"

She was wearing a beige hospital gown, creased and damp and not one of her best colors, but to him she'd never looked more beautiful. And he'd never loved her more.

He leaned over and kissed her cheek—wanting to kiss her lips, but not sure how that would be received.

Jordan had told him just minutes ago that Lacey was in love with him.

"She's never been in love before, Dermid. But she as much as admitted to me that she's in love with you. But she thinks it's hopeless...because of Alice."

"Why are you telling me?" Dermid asked, his mind a dizzy confusion of disbelief and hope as he tried to assimilate what Jordan had just said.

"She's my sister. I don't want to see her get hurt."

"I won't hurt her, Jordan. I promise you that."

And he intended to keep his promise, come what may.

Now, dragging a chair over to the bed, he sat down and focused his attention on his daughter. And felt his heart melt. Petite, dark-haired, dark-lashed, and creamy-cheeked, she was perfection. She was also asleep, making snuffly little sounds through her dear little tip-tilted nose, and even as he watched, she let Lacey's nipple slip from her mouth.

Lacey tucked her nightie back in place, but kept the baby snuggled against her breast.

"Does it make you sad," she asked quietly, "that it isn't Alice here with her?"

He traced a gentle fingertip over the baby's head. Eyes on the child, he said, "Thinking of Alice makes me sad. But it doesn't hurt the way it used to, and it hasn't in a while. Yes, it would have been wonderful if she could have had this baby herself, but it wasn't meant to be, and I accepted that a long time ago. Just as I accepted that when the baby was born, I'd be bringing her up alone."

"Dermid, I have something to tell you." Her voice

had a decided tremor and an edge of panic. ''Oh, this is so difficult for me to say, but—''

''You don't have to say it, Lacey.'' He looked at her, finally. ''I heard you as I came to the door, I heard you say you'd never give this baby away—''

''We've *bonded,* Dermid.'' Desperation shone in her eyes. ''I didn't mean for this to happen. I know I promised you I'd hand her over to you when she was born, I know I told you you need have no fears in that regard, it would be easy for me to walk away, but—'' her voice broke ''—I can't. I can't do it. I know she's Alice's baby...but she's mine, too. I love her already, I can't bear to part with her, and now that I've started breast-feeding her—''

''You don't have to part with her.''

She blinked. Stared at him bewilderedly. ''I don't?''

''I have a suggestion—''

But before he could explain, a nurse bustled in, bearing a small tray.

''Here's your tea, Ms. Maxwell. And the gel I mentioned.'' She set the tray on the bedside table, and after acknowledging Dermid with a pleasant nod, said, ''I'll take the baby now.''

She scooped the infant from Lacey's arms, and cradling her in her own, glanced at her and then glanced at Lacey and back again at the baby. ''She's very like you, Ms. Maxwell. She's going to be a great beauty, lucky little girl!''

Humming lightly, she bustled away again, leaving them alone.

"She's right," Dermid said. "Of course she's like you, I don't know why I didn't notice. It's not unusual for a child to look like someone else in the family, rather than like one of the parents. And the nurse was right, Gillian McTaggart is going to be a great beauty—"

"Dermid, you said you had a suggestion." Lacey lay back on her pillows, looking paler, he thought, than she had before. "What did you have in mind?"

She wasn't about to be sidetracked. She obviously wanted to get back to the matter on hand...which he did, too.

He cleared his throat. "I...um...thought...perhaps... you and I could get married."

A deathly silence, and then a shaky, nervous giggle. *"Married?"*

Was Jordan wrong? Did she not love him? He cleared his throat again. "I'm asking you to marry me." Hardly able to think straight, he barged on in a rush, "I'd like to make an honest woman of you—"

"But I've never been a *dis*honest woman, Dermid!"

"—and I'd like this baby to have a mom as well as a dad, and since you say you love her—"

"I do love her!"

"—you'll want to be closely involved in her life. You'll want to help bring her up—"

"Yes, I do, I do want to help bring her up—but you don't have to marry me!"

"Dammit!" he shouted, "I know I don't *have* to marry you. I *want* to marry you!"

She dug her teeth into her lower lip till it was as pale as her face. Then she said, lowering her gaze and speaking so quietly he had to strain to hear her, "To give the baby a mom."

"It's what you want, isn't it?"

"Yes, but—"

"Jordan told me you're in love with me." He hadn't meant to say it, the words had just come bursting out.

She winced as if he'd stabbed her. She rested a forearm across her eyes. "He shouldn't have said that."

"It isn't true, then?" His voice was thick with disappointment. She couldn't fail to have heard it. But he didn't care. Jordan had got it wrong, he thought with a pang of despair. Instead of warning him not to hurt Lacey, it should have been the other way around.

"Dermid?" She was peeking at him shyly from under her wrist. "Did you...*want* it to be true?"

There was a sparkle in her eyes that hadn't been there before, and it gave him a leap of hope. But not enough that he wasn't still cautious. "Do you *want* me to want it to be true?" he asked, and held his breath.

Her expression was mischievous. "Only if you want me to want you to want it to be true!"

It was back. The rapport they'd achieved before he left for Scotland was back. And he knew, then, that everything was going to be all right.

"Yes," he said. "I want it to be true because I love

you, I'm crazy about you, I can't live without you, and if you don't say you'll marry me—''

''I'll marry you, Dermid.'' She pushed herself up to a sitting position, and held out her arms. ''I'm madly in love with you, I'm crazy about you, too, and—''

But he kissed her before she could say any more. Kissed her till they were both out of breath, kissed her till he felt as if he was floating up to heaven. This was heaven. Being in love with Lacey and having her love him back was heaven.

There was only one more thing to say.

He took her shoulders and held her away a little. ''Lacey, about your career, about being the face of GloryB, I know how much that all means to you—''

''Don't, Dermid.'' She placed a fingertip over his lips. ''You don't have to say it. I know you'll expect me to stay home and be a full-time mom, just like Alice was—''

He circled her wrist with his fingers and pulled her hand down. ''Lacey, you're not like Alice. I don't expect you to be like Alice, I don't want you to be like Alice. You're Lacey, and the Lacey I fell in love with is not only a strong and courageous woman, who will be a wonderful mother to our little Jack and Jill, she's also a world-class model. Darling, you're going to be a modern mom, one who can cope beautifully with a career and a family because she has an adoring husband to back her up, one who wants to help, one who plans to help, one who's *incredibly* proud of her. You're going to have it all, Lacey. And I'm going to be on the sidelines, from start to finish, cheering you on.''

Lacey thought her heart might burst. How could she possibly be so lucky as to have this man love her?

''You're so good to me, darling Dermid.'' She kissed him, savouring the sweetness of his lips and the musky scent of his skin; and putting her arms around him, she sank against him, as the chemistry between them made her weak. ''And encouraging me to keep working, that's such a generous gesture. Beyond generous. But my family will always be my first priority and though being the face of GloryB will be thrilling, it'll also be my last major commitment. I can't think of anyplace in the world I'd rather be than at the ranch.''

He hugged her. ''Darling, you've made me happier than I ever thought possible. And I'm glad you'll be cutting back on your modeling, because I know how tough a job it must be.''

She reared back and quirked an amused eyebrow. ''Whatever happened,'' she asked, ''to the man who thought modeling was just a case of 'swanning around'?''

''When I saw how hard you worked to get my house running smoothly, and how determined you were when you taught yourself to cook, I realized that to get where you are in the modeling world, you must have given that same hundred percent of yourself. And I knew then that you weren't the sort of person to be satisfied with a job that entailed nothing but 'swanning around.'" He grinned. "Did I really refer to it as that?"

She laughed. "Yes, you did. More than once. But—" her face became serious "—there's one thing I must ask, Dermid. Why did you never miss a chance to needle me? Oh, I know that in the beginning you were just teasing, but later, after Alice died, your comments became sarcastic. And hurtful. It really upset me."

"Oh, my darling, I'm so sorry." He pulled her close, stroked her hair. "I didn't understand it myself, for a long time, but I've been thinking about it a lot lately, and I believe I do now. The teasing, that was the only way I knew how to relate to you. You were a model, you lived a glitzy life, jet-setting all over the place, you and I had no common ground. And then—you're right, and I'll always regret it—it later became mean. I think I resented you, resented the fact that while Alice had died you were still fluttering around, useless as a butterfly. I don't know at what point I started to become attracted to you, but the sarcasm then became a defence mechanism, to keep you at a distance. And it worked," he added ruefully. "It certainly kept us from getting to know each other—"

He cocked his head as the sound of quick light footsteps came from the corridor, followed by heavier steadier ones. A second later, Jack appeared in the open doorway, his brown hair disheveled, his hazel eyes alight.

"Hi, Aunt Lacey," he said. "I just got to see the

baby! When are you and me getting to take her home, Dad?''

As he spoke, Jordan and Felicity appeared behind him.

Dermid smiled and with his arm around Lacey's shoulder, said, ''It's not just you and I who are going to be taking home your baby sister, Jack. It's you and I and your aunt Lacey. Except she's not going to be only your 'Aunt Lacey' for much longer. As soon as I can get a wedding ring on her finger, she's going to be—''

''She's going to be my new *mom?*'' Jack gaped at Lacey.

Lacey beamed at him. ''Yes, darling, I am.''

Felicity's eyes opened wide...then sparkled with joy, while at the same time Jordan's mouth curved in a satisfied smile.

Dermid said, ''What do you think of that, son?''

Jack ran helter-skelter to the bed. ''What I think,'' he said, falling into Lacey's open arms, ''is I can't wait for you to get married so we'll be a real family!''

And Alice—who had watched over them all, unseen, from the beginning—now floated serenely away. As a rookie angel, this had been her first assignment, and though she'd been very nervous and had made more than her share of mistakes along the way, she was going to pass with flying colors, and she couldn't have been happier with the result.

She sighed a blissful sigh and looped a graceful loop.

It was truly going to be a marriage made in heaven!